The Sword of the Gray Queen 1:

Hunter of the Brilgura

Samuel Fleming

ii

Cover Art by MiblArt

ISBN-13: 978-1-954679-54-2 (paperback)
ISBN-13: 978-1-954679-53-5 (ebook)

This one's for Mom and Dad.

Thanks for always supporting me

and believing in me.

iv

Contents

"All that thrives in darkness
will burn in the light. That
which burns in the light,
garners no sympathy.
It deserves to burn."

—ENCHIRIDION:
Aurora Imperium, Principles.
Spread of Morning, Chapter 2.

Prologue

IDINA SAT MOTIONLESS on the field. It would be dawn soon. She was waiting for both the light of early morning and for her prey to wander in range of her longbow. She could just make out the silhouettes of a family of deer in the near-darkness.

Just a little closer.

The old hunter had camped on the outskirts of the swamp the last two mornings, hoping for an easy kill. It looked like today would be her day.

A few minutes later, a doe stood poised in the bleeding sunrise. Idina drew back her back, and the protests of the string seemed to echo across the field.

She loosed the arrow, and a moment later heard the dull thump of impact. The deer ran, but the doe dropped a moment later.

Idina sighed in relief and walked through the long grass. The doe lay dying on the ground—maybe lungshot. Idina was losing her touch.

She stooped and cradled the doe's head. Then she slipped her knife free and cut the doe's throat.

"Shh," Idina whispered. "Be still, now. *All is over, and the forest is quiet. Run where you wish and sleep where you may.*"

Idina wiped the blade clean and sheathed it. She would take it home, skin and butcher it. Half for the town, half for her.

She was about to grab the carcass to carry it home when she heard rustling across the field. The hunter looked up, staying crouched beneath the tall grass.

A figure was walking across the field—not fifty paces from her. It wore a dark cloak and carried something wrapped in a cloak over its shoulder.

Idina watched.

It wasn't the first morning she had seen the mysterious figure walking across the field. She knew it was one of the townfolk, but couldn't bring herself to confront them.

Twice, old Marl had complained about chickens going missing. Once, a young pig. This figure—whoever it was—was likely to blame. Had likely stolen another piglet this night.

Idina had seen magic before—she was no stranger to it. She'd seen it worked for good and for ill intentions. And so far in the town of Keld, there had been peace. If anything, sorcery might've been the reason their town had survived as long as it had.

Besides, Idina had her share of secrets, and she did not pry errantly at her neighbors.

So that morning, she merely watched from the grass as the figure strode into the swamp for whatever rites or magic it would summon.

It wasn't until the figure was at the threshold of the vines that a slender arm fell from the cloak.

~ ~ ~

Chapter 1
Folly of the Hunted

KEVRIL BERSK WANDERED into town looking rough and smelling worse. He had it on good authority that Winfield was sitting at the bar: On Archimedes' authority—the raven was staring through the window at the mark. One of Bersk's many abilities was being able to see through Archimedes' eyes—one of the least flashy, and most useful ones.

The bounty hunter had been off the road for nearly a week, catching up to his quarry. Chasing him through forests and across ruins of the old world. For the target's sake, his information better be worth it.

Bersk walked the short street to the bar, evening wind whipping at his cloak. He paid the locals absolutely no mind. The few he did pass knew to keep their mouths shut. Even the large blacksmith, who looked like he had coin to collect, had better sense than to look at Bersk sideways—at an unkempt man wearing spotless chainmail. Nobody but sellswords dressed in ragged clothes and magical armor.

And everyone knew not to cross a sellsword.

All the while, Bersk kept one eye on the road and one eye peering through Archimedes at the unsuspecting Winfield, who didn't realize that the raven had been following him for the last seven days and seven nights.

~

Kevril Bersk walked through the tavern door and saw himself through Archimedes's eyes. The bounty hunter shivered—one because it was always eerie to see himself like that and the second because—*Movernus*—he could *see* that he needed a bath. His long dark hair was matted and clung together, tan skin slick with sweat and grime.

Regardless, he kept looking through the bird's eye.

The tavern was nothing special, not in regards to taverns and certainly not in regards to other small town taverns. The dirt and sawdust on the floor was the same; as were the smells of sweat and spilled ale, and the downtrodden faces of the regular folk who hadn't the money nor the sense to leave for better parts.

But some of the people inside made this tavern different—the two capable-looking men by the entrance. Then there was the bartender—a retired sellsword turned barkeep named Manny. Still quicker with a blade than he was with a drink. The retired sellsword nodded ever so slightly to the still-employed one, glare shining off Manny's bald noggin.

Manny's eyes darted across the room to the two capable-looking men. Both well dressed, linens barely hiding chain and scale mail. Sword pommels peeking out from their cloaks. Both likely sellswords… Maybe they'd be willing to split the profit.

Today, it looked like it was just Manny that made this bar different.

Bersk the bounty hunter walked right up to Winfield and pulled out the closest chair to sit in. Then he leaned on the bar and eyed the man.

Winfield glanced in Bersk's direction, but quickly turned back to his ale, as if silence would do him any favors. He was stouter than Bersk would've guessed. At least his hands matched his work—thin fingers suited to a tailor. Sweat beaded on the mark's forehead and ran down his nose.

The bounty hunter tapped gloved fingers on the bar, the thuds echoing in the silence. "Guilty or just nervous?" Bersk asked, voice hoarse. Should've had an ale first.

Winfield smirked nervously and took a long drink, leaving foam across his upper lip. "Don't suppose it matters, does it?"

Bersk shrugged. "Wouldn't kill you to answer it."

Winfield glanced his way again, this time sizing Bersk up. Eyes lingering where the bounty hunter's sword *should* be.

Bersk snorted. "Don't even think about it. I still get paid if you're mostly alive." He swept back dark hair from his face and grinned.

"What information are they paying you for?"

Bersk thumbed the lodestone in his vest pocket. "Just a name. The name of the bishop."

Winfield perked up at that, eyes wide in a split second of fear before he took a long swig. Spilt ale bled down the glass and dripped onto the bar.

Winfield wiped his mouth on his sleeve. "You're with *them*, then?"

Them—the Order of Kripishi. The boogeymen most hadn't heard of and the rest wouldn't speak of. The sacred wing of the Church of First Light.

Bersk nodded. "The name," he said sternly. His patience was wearing thin. "The name and you go back on your merry way. A name, and five silver so I can get a room at the inn and a bath. Yeah, I say that would settle it."

Winfield didn't need much time, because he slipped a handful of silver from his pocket and made a show of dropping it on the bar. "Last chance," he said.

"That's my line," Bersk replied.

At that, the other two sellswords stood, hands on pommels.

Bersk sighed. Up until that moment, he thought the men might be willing to compromise—not that they'd been bought. Manny had given the wrong signal. "Some silver pieces to walk away?" he asked the men.

The stockier of the two gentlemen rolled a gold coin across his knuckles. "Gold spends better."

Bersk glanced back to Winfield. "And to think I let you off cheap."

The target shrugged and finished his beer, setting it down easy. He grabbed the edge of the bar, knuckles white—the look of a man about to turn around and run.

"Don't even think about it," Bersk whispered. "It'll be over quickly." Then he looked around to the dozen other regulars—all still and clutching their mugs of ale. "Now's the time to leave, if you be leaving."

A dozen chairs scraped the dirt. Half toppled over. In a span of two breaths, the bar was empty of patrons and mugs. The three sellswords stared each other down, while Winfield stared timidly at his own fingers.

From behind him Manny said, "You all best keep that *stercus* away from the bar."

"Last chance," the stocky mercenary said.

Bersk sighed, then whispered, "*Deprehendere magicae.*"

The two men's faces twisted in surprise at the old words. Both sellswords drew their weapons.

Bersk stood confidently. Neither of the men understood the words—if they had, they would've recognized a simple divination spell. He merely wanted to know if either man had magic weapons or armor—if they posed him any *real* danger.

Their ignorance of magic meant that they, in fact, posed him no threat at all.

The burly mercenary at least rushed Bersk with an experienced stance, the blade of his short sword resting on his off-hand gauntlet. The face of the second sellsword was twisted in false confidence, one belied by his gaunt frame, and two-handed, wild grip on his long-sword.

Through Archimedes' eye, Bersk saw Winfield still sitting at the bar, the corner of his lips raised in a smug grin as he held up a finger for another round of ale. The nerve.

Bersk held out his right hand, and with impossible suddenness and ghostly quiet, *Twitch* materialized in his hand. Its blade was deep blue and sickly curved, like the scaled horn of a dragon filed to deadly purpose. All he need do was will the sword to appear and no other force in the world could slow its return. The sword was his alone to command.

In the next breath, the big sellsword's eyes went wide and his steps slowed. He knew little of magic, but knew enough to recognize the feat or the blade, or both. He stopped in his tracks and his sword-hand fell.

Bersk turned from Winfield to the young mercenary, and as he swung down wild with the long sword, Bersk parried and it fell harmlessly to the right. Before the man could swing back, or even stop his charge, Bersk leaned his left elbow into the sellsword's jaw. The fight and his feet went out from under the lad and the next he saw, he was looking up from the floor. The long sword on the ground, out of reach.

Through Archimedes' eyes, Bersk saw Winfield turn to run. The bounty hunter stuck out a foot and caught his leg, sending the man sprawling across the floor.

Bersk's sword was trained on the young mercenary, who was still reeling from the impact.

"Please don't kill him," the older sellsword said. He sheathed his sword, using two hands to hide the trembling in his arms. "We didn't know. We didn't know."

Bersk looked back down to the bested mercenary, willed his magic sword away with the same blink that it arrived, offered a hand to the lad and pulled him up. It was only then that Bersk saw the resemblance in the men—close enough to be brothers. The young mercenary backed away quickly, blood trickling down his nose, defiant look gone from his eye.

"Don't forget your sword," Bersk said. "Go on."

The lad grabbed it meekly and then Bersk picked up Winfield by the shirt collar and sat him back down at the bar.

"Go on home and live another day," Bersk said to the stunned sellswords. He turned his back to them and sat back down with the mark. "Don't worry. Winfield will make it back home, too. His pockets are a little lighter for it, but his gold bought you men something valuable today."

"What is that, sir?" the young sellsword asked, hand to his nose.

"That men such as me are rarely kind. Next time you meet my like they will cut you down without a thought."

With that, the two mercenaries had the sense to leave. The elder of the two mumbled a thank you as the door shut behind them.

Bersk had streaks of kindness because he could afford it. Because when poor thugs or feeble mercenaries came after him, most recognized when they were bested. He imagined it was much the same quick and deep-seated realization when those men looked at a dire bear or a dragon. Unfortunately, mages such as him were callous for much the same reason—because they could afford to be.

Magic set him apart. Most knew to avoid it. And those who didn't know, learned quickly.

Kevril Bersk reached to the pile of silver pieces on the bar and pushed one over to the trembling target.

"Go on… order that drink," Bersk said, voice falling heavy in the empty bar. "Two of them."

~

Manny pulled two full ales and passed them to Winfield and to Bersk. No one else had come into the bar, not since the two sellswords left so quickly. Bersk doubted anyone else would come, not until they saw the bounty hunter and his target leave.

Bounty Hunters and sellswords were almost as bad for a tavern's business as a priest.

Bersk let the man take a swift swig before he reminded him of business. "The name of the bishop." He thumbed the lode-stone in his vest pocket with his ungloved hand.

Winfield glanced his way again before taking another long swig. "I'm going to need another beer, I'm afraid."

"You're going to need the john," Manny said with a quick smile. The bartender and retired sellsword glanced to the one who was still working for approval. "What do you say?"

Bersk shook his head. "No name. No more ale. Too many drinks and good Winfield might get the courage to say the wrong one."

Winfield chuckled nervously and slowly spun his mug on the bar. "Either way, I'm a dead man. Wrong name or right."

"That's between you, the Lord, and the Church."

With trembling lips, he answered, "Santa Anna."

Breath caught in Bersk's throat and the bounty hunter forced himself to breathe. "Now it's my turn to tell you *last chance*. Are you sure—"

"Yes." Winfield closed his eyes. Thin tears fell from the corners. Meanwhile, Manny dried glasses and pretended to look uninterested.

"Go on," Bersk said. "Get out of here."

Winfield turned to the bounty hunter, now with eyes wide and red. "Don't tell them. You mustn't tell them."

"I work for the Church. I don't decide their business." Bersk let go of the lodestone and felt it warm in his pocket. Soon the church would know. All of them would know. He grasped his mug of ale and drank a swig to put it behind him. "To Santa Anna," he said, and wiped the froth from his lips, trying to hide the pit in his stomach.

Winfield stood solemnly, staring at Bersk, but the bounty hunter would not meet his eyes. "You've damned her. Fed her to the wolves—"

"Get out," Bersk seethed. "Before you find the limits of my mercy."

Winfield left without another word, leaving Kevril Bersk alone with what he had done. Alone with Manny drying the damn mugs.

"You can cut that out now," Bersk said before taking a long draw of ale. Despite the glove that was supposed to cover his sensitive right hand, he could feel the slightest movement of the bubbles. It was acting up earlier and earlier as of late, and the bounty hunter switched hands.

"You really ought to get that looked at," Manny said, raising an eyebrow and nodding to Bersk's gloved hand. "And cut what out?"

"Pretending to look disinterested," the bounty hunter added, ignoring his comment. "And what was with that earlier? You gave me the *they got your back* nod, not the *target has back up* nod."

"Oh, this?" Manny held up the limp rag. "I got this next to your *I'm just a weapon of the Church* sap. You don't work for them anymore, Bersk." He kept drying.

"I do," Bersk said sternly. He waffled between trying to explain *again* that he was not a Knight of the Order anymore and that he still owed some of the Bishops favors, before finally settling on, "It's complicated."

"Uh huh," was all Manny said in reply. Somehow, the old sod kept finding pieces to dry. During his *working days,* Manny supposedly polished his knives with the same tik and dedication.

What *could* Bersk do, really? The Church of First Light wanted an answer and they would find out sooner or later, whether they sent him or someone with less tact.

Even if he wanted to do something, even if he wanted to make a dramatic stand—to say, *not Santa Anna. It couldn't be*—they would barrel over him like the Church did everything else. It was more like those Elven machines than it was the will of the Lord.

So he would sit here and drink a few moments, surrounded by peace and wracked by inner turmoil. Oftentimes, that was all a man could do.

"So that's it then?" Manny said, finally ceasing with the mugs. He sat one down loudly on the bar for punctuation. "You're going to leave her to the Church?"

"Yep."

"That poor girl—"

"She's no girl anymore," Bersk corrected. "She's *a bishop*. And she hasn't been found guilty. She's just suspect. She'll get a trial—which is a right better than the lot get. Hopefully, she's innocent and Winfield is very, very mistaken...."

"Or?" Manny asked, staring at him intently. "You trailed off there, Bersk."

The mercenary squinted at Manny. "There's nothing to solve here, ol' sellsword. Just go back to wiping those mugs."

A smirk flashed across Manny's face, glare shining off his teeth and the top of his head. He turned back to his bartenderly duties and mumbled, "Oh, you're no fun."

Bersk hid his own smirk with a drink.

What he had been about to say was: *Or Santa Anna was guilty. That she knowingly went against the Church.* Which would cause a whole mess of trouble for her, the Church, the Lord...

And for Kevril Bersk.

~

Kevril Bersk nursed his ale for a quarter of an hour in relative peace. He leaned heavy on the bar and turned the mug around slowly on the dark wood. The waltz of the mug helped to quiet his mind. At some point, Manny lit a cigar and sat on a stool behind the bar—Bersk only noticed once the smell of smoke and cloves had wafted in his direction.

Between the ale, the quiet, and turning the mug—peace, if only for a while. Nothing lasts forever in this world.

The regulars came back too, their need for drink overpowering their fear. They stopped, one by one, at the end of the bar opposite Bersk and retreated to further reaches of the tavern.

Then a figure walked up beside him. "An ale, Manny," said the smooth, deep voice to his right. Bersk recognized it right away. "Well, well, Blink. Fancy seeing you here."

Bersk paused mid-drink. "You don't get to call me that."

Tam thanked Manny for the drink, then made a point of sitting two seats away from him. "You need a shower, Kev."

Bersk leaned back in his chair and regarded his accomplice. From any other soul, the comment would've come as an insult, but Tamren Jorbough was a bard and a poet, and mid-life with experience. One with a voice that could sell insurrection to a king. He was of unassuming build, draped in a deep red sash and silk shirt. Not as gaudy as his stage outfits, but then the bard didn't come to a wee town such as this to perform—there wasn't enough coin here to afford him.

"You don't get to call me that either," Bersk said.

Tam frowned. "I don't get to call you Blink—"

"You haven't seen the trick."

The bard gestured to Bersk's right hand. "I've seen the sword."

From behind the bar, Manny paused with the towel and quipped, "That's not the trick," before setting to polishing again.

Tamren sighed, "Well then, why can't I call you Kev?"

Bersk finished off his mug. "*Women* call that."

Tam shrugged, "Bersk it is then. I'm no better than the common rabble."

Manny added, "*I* call him Bersk."

The bard squinted at the bartender. "But have you seen the trick?" Manny nodded slyly. "Well, it's settled. I'll just have to stick by your side long enough to see the trick or to retire."

An infectious smile had grown on the men's faces. It belied a bond forged by men in a dangerous profession—a mutual understanding that, in fact, they were friends, and that they would be lucky to see such a day as *retirement*.

Also, that Tamren Jorbough was one of the few men that could've survived calling the bounty hunter by Kev, if it were not for two things: That so far only intimate relations had called him his shortened name, and that Bersk had heard Tam seduce far too many with his voice—to the point that it was hard to keep a straight face when the bard used the name.

Thankfully, Tam dropped the topic to regale them of his latest show in the theater of New Chessi.

"The city is returning to its former glory," Tam said. The bard stroked his long beard as he talked, an idle habit. "It's been twenty years, but you can hardly tell that it was razed to the ground. The streets were covered in petals and everlit candles floated all around. The mayor asked me to write two songs for the occasion. *Two*, I said. Two... He certainly thought New Chessi was worthy of it."

"I'm sure your songs were worthy," Bersk added.

"Oh yes, yes. The choir and I made a brilliant quartet. They were absolutely smitten with me after the second song. They *insisted* on accompanying me the rest of the evening."

"Three?" Manny mumbled from behind the bar, towel paused in mental math.

Tam nodded coyly. "Absolutely breathtaking."

Bersk waved a dismissive hand. "Surely you haven't come to gloat."

Tam raised an eyebrow. "Gloat? Me? I would never, not to Kevril Bersk, blade of the Church, last hope of the wicked, last breath of the righteous; thrown away more chances with damsels, wenches, maidens and princesses than a mere mortal such as I!"

Manny turned away—rolling his eyes at the lines. "Here we go again."

Bersk rubbed his temple. "One time. It was one time. I try to intimidate some bandits—"

Tam looked offended. "Hey, it was a good line. It worked. They desecrated their breeches!"

Bersk interjected, "Tam, the line was *the last hope of the righteous, last breath of the wicked.*"

"No, no, that doesn't make sense," the bard said, wagging a finger. "The maidens are breathless and the wicked are repenting."

The bounty hunter chuckled and looked to Manny, but the barkeep still had his back turned, shoulders bouncing, and a hand to his mouth to stifle the laughter. Manny was no help— he was retired.

"So, you didn't come to gloat," Bersk reminded the bard, trying to herd the poet back onto topic.

Tamren's eyes widened, and he stroked his beard again. "Yes, yes. I've found some business for you in a little town two or was it three days North. A little town that calamity forgot… Missing livestock here and there. Now, missing children." The bard leaned heavy on the bar at that before continuing. "They didn't give me much to relay, not even when I told them I knew a monster hunter."

Bersk slammed his ale and pushed away from the bar.

"Where are you going?" the bard asked.

The bounty hunter shrugged. "Was that it?" Tam nodded sheepishly, and Bersk continued, "Then I'm going to get a room and then a bath. We leave at first light. Good evening, gentlemen." He took five silver coins and left the rest on the bar. "Manny, always a pleasure."

~

Both the bard and barkeep nodded, and Kevril Bersk strode out of the tavern.

Archimedes flew to his left shoulder. Its nails dug into the bounty hunter's cloak and leather vest beneath. The raven cooed and Kevril ruffled the top of its head. There Archy stayed, silent and attentive, while the bounty hunter walked across town to the inn.

The bird was bound to him, as was the sword. Unfortunately, Archimedes couldn't disappear like Twitch could and few shopkeeps appreciated the raven's presence.

So, Kevril Bersk bid the raven to wait on the roof while he talked to the lanky couple that ran the inn. For two extra silver pieces, they set him up in a corner room and drew him a luke-warm bath.

Kevril wedged *Twitch* against the door so that the hilt was against the door knob and the blade was pointed down. When he was satisfied the door was barred, he opened up the window and let Archimedes in. Then bid the raven to watch the window while he bathed.

And the bounty hunter steeped, letting the weight leave him first. Then when he was properly relaxed, he washed himself, taking care not to submerge his right hand. An old injury had left his forearm and hand disfigured—the skin was paper thin and the muscle frayed and wiry, giving length from the elbow to fingertips a ghoulish and unnatural look. Thanks to the magic of the Church, the arm was completely usable and without any loss of function, though it was horrendously sensitive to touch and temperature. So to spare himself and onlookers, his right hand never saw the light of day.

Oddly enough, the magic sword was one of the few things that his hand was not overly sensitive to.

His clothes were last to wash and then hung to dry. It was about as relaxing of an evening as a sellsword could get—certainly the most relaxed Kevril had been in days. He drifted off to sleep in the scratchy sheets, thinking about what it could possibly be like to retire like Manny had—should Kevril be lucky enough to live that long.

Archimedes watched the window, without sleep, worry or complaint.

~ ~ ~

Chapter 2
Highwaymen

KEVRIL BERSK WOKE at first sun from a dreamless sleep. Both Archimedes and *Twitch* were where he left them. He dressed in silence, then willed the sword to disappear and the bird to his left shoulder. Then the bounty hunter walked out of his room and down the short hall to find the bard. He rapped on the door three times, to which Tam groaned. Then Bersk waited outside in the morning air.

Tamren walked out a few minutes later, weary of the morning sun but without complaint. No doubt he was used to keeping an evening-tilted schedule. The bard wore his same sash and shirt. He carried a small pack over his shoulder and a lute painted deep green with white swirls. For such a noble appearance, he traveled light, owing much to the use of magic to fill the gaps: A costume gifted by the elves, one which could become any manner of design and color, even so far as changing the location of seams. And rather mundane magic to take the smell and stain out of his clothes, cutting down on bathing or spices to cover up a few too many nights on the road.

No doubt a striking contrast to his counterpart—Kevril Bersk donned mostly blacks and grays, apart from his chainmail, greaves, and shoulder pauldrons, which flashed a deep silver. Black had become a staple; it didn't stand out, *and* it was easy to look clean.

The pair paid silver for two brown horses and provisions for horse and man, then set off North for Keld. Luckily, there was a road that would take them all the way there. It wasn't safe to travel off-road—even though Bersk had spent the last week doing just that—since unsavory creatures lurked away from civilization. It wasn't a trouble the bounty hunted wanted to revisit.

The roads were a different kind of trouble. Bandits and soldiers, mostly. The occasional vicious bear or wyvern.

If the stories were true, the roads had only grown more dangerous in recent decades after Sircius Everdeath destroyed half the continent. There had been a resurgence across the countryside of both man and beast, and the road was where they collided.

Because of that, travelers and merchants stuck to caravans. Numbers, as well as a healthy number of guards and crossbows, kept most peril at bay.

But then, the worst of the creatures never ventured to the roads. They stayed confined to the woods, to their bastions of horror, content to wait for the foolish to wander into their domain. Kevril Bersk knew this because he hunted those things—the worst of them. He was their bane, their last breath.

The question now was, what horror had the town of Keld stumbled upon? Or what horror had they unwittingly brought back with them?

~

The first day passed uneventfully, save for the glares of a passing merchant caravan. Crossbow boltheads were embedded in the side boards, shafts broken off near-flush with the wood. Other wounds were older, bolts completely removed. Their wagon creaked and groaned, heavy with cargo. If it were bandits, then the caravan fared well.

The driver and some of the soldiers in front, all wearing red regalia, spit on the ground as the bard and bounty hunter passed.

"Lovely crowd tonight," Tamren scoffed. He rode slightly behind and to the right of Bersk as they passed on the narrow street.

"Any you remember?" Bersk asked in jest. Tam had already gone across the road once to the village and come back by lodestone.

The bard shook his head.

"I'm sure we'll run into prettier ones later," Bersk replied, hair whipping in the breeze. He gave the soldiers as little thought as he gave the townsfolk—less even. At least the townsfolk would help you for coin. The soldiers wouldn't help you, even if you were bleeding on their boots.

The prettier ones Bersk referred to were the mercenaries down the road. The same that had set upon the caravan. They were likely still there, and if they were that brazen, likely in the same spot. Luckily, the bard had taken Bersk's meaning without him having to spell out the joke.

Tam chuckled nervously. "Right. Well, that's what you're for. Perhaps I'll finally see how you got that nickname."

Blink.

The bounty hunter smirked. "If I have to resort to that… Then things have gotten dire, and you better have an equally impressive trick up your sash."

Archimedes flew above them, circling in wide, sweeping arcs. The raven's eyes were much better than Bersk's—good enough to see both a wide field and spot single predators from nearly a mile away. But the bounty hunter needn't peer through his familiar's eyes all the time. The pair's minds were linked so that Archimedes could subtly alert him to danger; not even a caw was necessary. For now, Archimedes was his silent, tireless guardian.

~

That evening, when the sun began bleeding orange into the sky, they camped just off the road and under the relative cover of a giant doddler tree. Bersk set to digging a fire pit to take the chill of the night air, while the bard tied and tended to the horses. Archimedes perched high in a dead tree.

"Are you sure we can't rest under another tree?" Tam asked. The bard stopped scooping horse feed and wiped his eyes. "The pollen of these flowers is fierce."

"Exactly why we're stopping here. Most creatures can't stand the pollen."

"Then how are you not sniffling? Did you sell your soul to the doddler trees?"

Bersk smiled. Sweat beaded on his forehead, but the hunter didn't slow. He was nearly finished digging. "Merely spent too many nights on the road. Besides, I'm pretty sure I lost my soul to the Church."

"I don't think that's how that works."

"And what do you know of the Church?"

The bard finished feeding the horses, wrapped the feed bag tight, then set to unfurling their bedrolls. "What else do you think I'm doing on those late evenings? Spreading the good word of course."

Bersk chuckled. The hole was finished, and he set to gathering wood for the fire. Twitch made the task easy—where it lacked in weight, it more than made up for in sharpness. Bersk felled two thick branches from Archimedes' dead tree before he paused to ask the bard, "You don't believe, do you?"

Tamren was already laying on his bedroll, hands behind his head and wide-brimmed hat down over his eyes. "Come now, you can't ask questions such as that when you're not lying intimately next to someone."

"I prefer to know those things *before* lying intimately next to someone."

"And bless you, Kevril Bersk. But I've found Terrans are at their most truthful after fornicating."

The bounty hunter willed Twitch away and carried an armful of twigs and thin-sliced logs to the pit. "Surely you could get most of your mark's secrets without sleeping with them."

Tam tipped his hat and grinned. "Why would I deny myself such an obvious perk of the job?"

Bersk's attention was torn away. Archimedes saw six figures approaching from the road. They walked on foot along the edge of the woods, some quarter mile away.

The bounty hunter set the bundle of kindling in the pit and stood to regard the lounging entertainer. "Then I ask again, having already camped beside you on the road."

Tam propped himself up on an elbow and pushed his hat back. "Very well, Kevril Bersk. I'll tell you what I believe. I believe that the legend of Movernus has been around since before Terrans had the will or the sense to write about things.

The Church's Lord is a recent invention. I'm fond of the old masters and the classics. They're classics for a reason, you know." The bard said this with a mix of carefree and seriousness—mixed, as truth often came. Then Tam added, "Don't stop with the fire on account of me."

Bersk crossed his arms. "Things I do, I do for a reason." He nodded up to the road. "Highwaymen approach from the North…"

He bid Archimedes fly closer and settle in on the branches. Bersk wanted a good look at the men, for that would inform their fate. In the twilight, the raven saw the world in perpetual gray. The nuance of color escaped, but all other details were laid bare: The men were ragged and weary-eyed as they scanned the treeline. There was no doubt to their purpose, for they carried no belongings, save for the plain swords in their hands. Their own camp was likely along the road. One man carried a crossbow with only three bolts in his quiver—which meant they were running low on supplies.

The bard rose to a crouch. He whispered, "What does Archimedes see?"

The sellsword sighed. "Weary men who should not wander along such a dangerous stretch of road."

The poor and destitute often resorted to thievery, but often they could be nudged to a more righteous path. Bersk wasn't pompous enough to think that he could do this. Too often Terrans did not listen to one another, no matter how potent the advice. Fate and circumstance were far more effective.

As for the weary highwaymen, their pillaging along this stretch of road had led them to a nightmare.

First, he bid Archimedes to speak and the skillful raven made not just words, but an entire scene unfold in the darkness. Its caw became crunching leaves, breaking saplings, then it became the pounding of heavy footsteps. A man's panicked voice echoed through the night, *"Run, gods. No—"* followed by his dying scream. Sounds of bones and flesh splitting.

By now, the highwaymen were clustered together and backing away from the treeline. Bersk and Tam had turned toward the vicious, hidden scene.

But sounds wouldn't be enough. The men needed to see.

He bid Archimedes to change into its Ugu form. The unassuming raven flitted to the ground, the rustle of leaves barely registered by the highwaymen just thirty feet away. Archimedes grew.

Tam grabbed at his bounty hunter's shirt sleeve. "What is it, Bersk? What's out there?" Tam pleaded.

Using such magic weakened Bersk's connection to his guardian. His vision and command grew fleeting. So Bersk described the abomination from memory as Archimedes took form. "The beast is hunched and massive. Its skin is thick and mottled with reddish brown fur, belying coiled muscles. Its shoulders stand eight feet tall and nearly as wide across the chest—weighing as much as three horses, with proportions large enough to grasp a man with one hand around the torso and crush him like a grape. The face alone is hairless, the skin taut and bone-white. Its eyes are wide, void black, and unblinking, like the eyes of a child's doll. Its teeth are filed sharp with great tusks that split the gums on either side."

Tam's grip grew tighter around Berk's sleeve, while the bounty hunter's grip grew tenuous on Archimedes. Kevril Bersk commanded two more things of the Ugu: *Scare them, but spare them death and grievous injury. Return when you smell shit.*

The Ugu erupted from the treeline, its feet and knuckles shook the ground. The highwaymen screamed in shrill terror and ran. Most of their steps grew distant and were cut off by the scream of the lone man that the beast grabbed by the leg. He whimpered and pawed at the cobblestones as he was dragged across the ground, back through the brush and bramble.

"Oh, Movernus," Tam whispered. "Bersk… Bersk…"

Bersk heard the scene—seeing glimpses of terror from the screaming highwaymen. Bersk did not need to narrate to the shaking bard, for the sounds and Tam's own imagination would bring much greater terror.

The bard was no doubt expecting the sounds of a grisly fate… but none would befall the man. Not that night.

They heard a man running through the woods and across the road; the sounds of a highwayman trying desperately to catch up his accomplices.

The shaking and pounding of the beast vanished as the psychopomp changed back into its raven form.

Poor Tam's grip slackened, and he scooted feebly backward, imagination no doubt conjuring all manner of end for them.

Bersk hid his grin.

As Tam's breathing grew hoarse, Archimedes soared through the clearing.

Tam watched the raven with wide eyes as it looped in the air and landed on the bounty hunter's shoulder, then promptly collapsed back on his bedroll.

~

When Bersk was sure that Tam's heart hadn't stopped from fright, the bounty hunter started laughing silently and breathlessly. The raven cawed in much the same manner.

Tam laid there, shaking his head quietly in shock and disbelief. "You son of a winking duck," he mumbled. "You club-footed albino bastard. Was… Was that Archimedes the whole blasted time!" When Bersk's laughter hadn't subsided in the slightest, Tam added. "I thought that was it. Movernus had come to whisk me away."

"Come on, Tam," Bersk said, wiping his eyes and bidding Archimedes back up to his perch in the trees. "I was merely giving you ideas for your next song."

"Oh, that's a right poor excuse. What shall I make of that? *Come hear a tale of terror and dread, of bounty hunter's ploy misread. Here lies Tamren Jorbough, Bard of Bakersfield, tried to flee but shit instead.*" The bard finally relaxed, though stayed on the bedroll. "My breeches are alright, by the way—but real life must be embellished for song."

Bersk winced, stomach already tight from laughing. He didn't tell his comrade that he fared better than some. With any luck, out there in the night were six highwaymen who would give up their thieving ways for more honest trades, far from the horrors of the road.

~ ~ ~

IDINA EMERGED FROM the swamp, ragged and breathless. She'd searched all morning for the mysterious figure and the child it had carried into the swamp.

She'd found neither.

She barely remembered searching—

Barely remembered staggering back to her house—collapsing on the ground outside.

Idina sobbed until her chest and her face ached, until her fingers were numb.

At some point, villagers from Keld had come across the field looking for the child. Somewhere beyond her sorrow, Idina heard their angry shouts, felt the rage bearing down on her. The mob saw Idina and seized her. She didn't fight them.

How could she fight? She was too late.

She hadn't found the strength then, and she wouldn't find it now.

She had failed.

Rather than string her up, the mob took her to the small jail in the center of town. Idina would've been surprised if she wasn't in shock.

The old hunter leaned against the cold stone of the jail cell, her wrist and ankle chains clinking. Outside, men yelled.

"Burn her!"

"Hang her!"

"Nothing will be done to her!" Reynold's voice—the town elder. The mob fell to discordant grumbling.

Only as things quieted did Idina stop sobbing. She felt as if she had no tears left to cry.

Idina slumped against the wall like a broken blade. Of all the things she had seen in her life, why had this wracked her so? Why had she hesitated?

Why had she been afraid? The old hunter breathed slowly, trying to steady herself.

She was wrong, she still had tears left to cry.

~ ~ ~

Chapter 3
The Town of Keld

THE OTHER TWO days and nights on the road passed uneventfully, much to the bard's relief. No more monsters. No more bandits. Only subdued tales of excitement from both men and two songs from the bard—both that Bersk had heard before: *The Ballad of Bellasandra Liesl* and *East of Drowned.*

Some men were fond of retelling old jokes. Tamren Jorbough was fond of replaying the same songs. This wasn't a problem, at least for the songs that Tam wrote—for the bard was a stellar minstrel—but he had a habit of butchering other's lyrics.

~

The pair came upon the pastures first, stalks of oats and grain waving in the afternoon breeze on the fourth day. Bersk had bought extra grain and rations, for if there was one other thing he could count on Tam for, it was miscalculating distance.

Archimedes followed high in the sky, circling in wide arcs. Sellswords were rare, and likely to spook folk when they came into town—sent for or not. Sellswords with trained animals were rarer still, and Bersk was set on not making a scene first thing upon coming to town.

From the sky, Bersk looked down through the Raven's eyes and saw the place for what it was. Tam had called Keld a town, but it was little more than a village surrounded by woods and a swamp to the West. A dozen families or so, living and working and minding each other, and not a perimeter wall to hide behind. The kind of place folk were born in, survived in, and died in. The kind of quiet life that folk either ran from or hobbled to.

And the sellsword and the bard stuck right out. Stares came from the fields at first, then the dwellings as they passed into the heart of the village. Thatched roofs rose out of the landscape and townsfolk along with them.

The first to stop them were farmers returning from whatever passed for a market. The young couple rode together at the head of the wagon, a graying horse in front, and a quarter load of carrots and greens in the back. Though the husband drove and stopped the horse, it was his wife that greeted them.

"Back again, minstrel?" she asked, squinting at him from beneath her bonnet.

"Why yes, madam. I've come back with one Kevril Bersk," Tam said proudly, waving a hand to his comrade. "He'll see to your monster problem."

She looked the hunter up and down and nodded in subtle approval. "Truth be told, we didn't think you'd be back minstrel, with how quick you left town the other day... It means a lot that you sent for him so quickly. You mustn't have slept a wink since you left."

Tam brought a hand to his chest. "I couldn't sleep knowing that such trouble befell you."

At this, the husband turned sheepishly. "Sir, would you kindly play for the town again? After dealing with the monster, of course. It was… Well, it was sorely needed after the season we've had."

Bersk interjected, "I'm sure the bard would *love* to do so again. He is a man of the people. And I'm sure he would do so at no charge." The simultaneous joy of the villagers and the stifled surprise of the bard were two sides of the same shining coin.

The couple expressed their heartfelt thanks before departing.

"*No charge…*" Tam mumbled. In spite of his obvious frustration, the bard forced a smile, for there were still people watching from elsewhere on the street.

"Think of the good your songs will do. You'll cure the anguish that my blade cannot."

"I've never worked for so little."

"What about that little town near Winterfrain, the Mages College in Hammerdin, or your hometown?"

Tam held out his fingers as he tallied his response. "The first paid in ale, the mages paid me in secrets, and I was an apprentice back then. Did you even listen to that story? Apprentices don't get paid. I was doing it for the practice and for the *exposure*." Tam sneered the last word for emphasis, his guarded facade flickering at the word.

"Funny way of saying free," Bersk replied, echoing the line Tam had used *every time* he told that story.

Tam glanced his way, a smirk flashing across his lips. "And that was the last time I worked for exposure."

"Come on, then," Bersk said, spurring his horse onward. "We best find this monster and get you playing. I'll ask the elder to toss a few silvers in your hat."

"Right, right. So long as it's only a few coins. They're already paying you." Tam followed beside him, pointing the way toward the elder's house.

Bersk shrugged. He took payment when he could get it. Most people hadn't the coin to pay the wages for his talents. This hadn't much mattered when he worked for the Church of First Light, since they provided a stipend and rarely asked for tidings.

That was part of why he continued taking the occasional odd job from select contacts in the Church. He owed them favors, sure, but they paid for his troubles. That, in turn, allowed him to wander the continent with a little more freedom that he'd had when he officially served the Lord.

~

Small towns like Keld didn't have shops, so much as they had families that ran them. Most children followed in the professions of their parents, and Keld was no different. The sellsword and the bard passed an empty long building that likely doubled as a church and as a school—school was secondary to living. Learning the family trade was far more important.

As such, children peered out from the houses, pausing whatever they were working on. The sooty face of the blacksmith's kid, the tailor's kid clutching a ball of string, the cobbler's kid holding a single shoe.

Tam steered them around a small bend in the row and proclaimed they'd arrived at the elder's home, scarcely different from the others.

"Are you sure this is the right place?" Bersk asked as they dismounted.

Tam nodded and rapped on the door while Bersk tied their horses to the stake.

A young man answered the door and a gruff voice beckoned from behind him. Bersk and Tam stepped to the threshold of the cobbler's hovel. The smell of leather and flour hung in the air. The main room was filled with simple shoes, drying leather and packed with people: Two girls stepping in a tub to soften the leather, the oldest lad slicing strips of it. Mother and father stitching leather to the wood sole. Eyes flitted to the bard and the sellsword, but none turned away from their tasks for long.

After a moment, the man stood wearily and introduced himself as Reynolds. He was heavy set, with graying stubble and sharp features. He kissed his wife's forehead, then bid the men to step outside to talk.

Reynolds breathed deep when they stepped outside. "I'd rather not discuss things in front of the children. Good a reason as any to step out and stretch the legs." He turned and led them from curious stares across to the other side of town.

They walked to the outskirts, to where fields started again and where the ruin of a large dwelling lay. It was little more than a burnt outline and rubble. Remnants of a brick chimney stood waist high like a grave marker. They walked right into the middle of it, stepping over the edges and onto rubble.

Reynolds hooked his thumbs on his suspenders. "So, where should I start?"

Bersk said, "How about the beginning."

Reynolds nodded meekly. "Best we figure, it all started a few weeks ago. Livestock going missing in the middle of the night. At first it was chickens, then hogs. A few of us stayed up one night to see if it was foxes or wolves, but it was a person. Wearing a black cloak. We chased them off, and they ran toward the hunter's den down there by the swamp. We figured we had the hunter pegged, so we drug her out of her house and locked her up here in town…" He trailed off, then wiped his nose.

"But that wasn't the end, was it?" Bersk asked.

Reynolds shook his head. "No. It stopped for three nights, then… Then Sven went missing. Vanished. No older than seven. We went back to the cabin, to the swamp. We didn't make it far inside… There were bones sticking out of the muck. Chicken, pig, and the little boy's skeleton hanging from the vines." The man brought a hand to his face, breath catching in his throat.

Bersk and Tam waited for Reynolds to compose himself before the elder continued. "We've been keeping watch at night, but we haven't seen anyone else."

The sellsword and the bard exchanged a glance, questions forming in both their minds. Tam stroked his beard and then gestured for Bersk to go first.

"Tell me about the swamp," Bersk said. "Legends, history, anything that comes to mind."

Reynolds looked off toward the swamp with apprehension. It loomed two miles away on the edge of town, a dark smudge of green and brown beyond the fields.

"There's many a story, knight. There's the troll brothers who gobble up children after dark, Bellasandra the vampyre who lusts after the blood of adulterers, or the scaled troglodyte." Reynolds frowned. "They're… They're all just stories.

There's probably wolves or bears or some ungodly creature in there, but no one here knows for sure. The townsfolk mostly steer clear of it. All 'cept for the hunter. That's her house there on the edge of it. When we looked for the boy… That was the first I'd seen of it. If the gods are kind, that will be the last of it too."

Though the elder didn't believe in those monsters, Bersk knew there was always a shred of truth in legends—even if it was as simple as a man-eating wolf or dire-bear living in the swamp. Of the legends, none seemed plausible. A Troglodyte would never venture out of the swamp and vampyres left mummified corpses instead of bones. Besides, the Bellasandra of the old songs was long dead. Trolls hated other trolls and so the idea of brothers was absurd, though a single troll was a possibility. But then there was the cloaked figure…

Tam asked, "What about the hunter? We should question her. See what she knows."

Reynolds's face soured again. "She's locked up."

"Still? Why?" the bard asked.

"We haven't seen the cloaked figure since we locked her up. Most folk think she's to blame."

Tam stroked his beard again. "It could be that the boy wandered off. Heard rumors in the town about the hunter and the swamp."

Bersk said, "You don't sound convinced."

Tam shook his head subtly. "I'm just speculating."

The sellsword turned to Reynolds. "We'll need to speak with the hunter."

Reynolds looked to the town, then back to the men. "I'll arrange it… But you must hurry. They're talking of hanging the woman."

Kevril Bersk laid a hand on the elder's shoulder. "Do you believe she's guilty?"

"No."

"Then you must implore the township to wait."

"Why?"

Bersk replied, "Because you may be right, and they may put an innocent woman to death. Because there's still a man-eater living in that swamp and I may need the hunter's aid. Lastly— and listen close—some creatures are bound to a master, and I may need the master alive to deal with the creature. Do you understand me?"

Reynolds nodded, eyes wide with dismay and understanding.

"Good," Bersk said, removing his hand. "Take us to the hunter."

~

Reynolds led the sellsword and the bard back through town. Through Archimedes's eyes, Bersk saw a crowd of a dozen men gathering in the center—in such a small town, it was likely *most* of the men. They were armed with pitchforks and swords. The sellsword bid Archimedes to land on the closest building, a squat, plain thing that couldn't hold more than two cells. None of the men noticed the raven perched nearby.

"Is the jail around the corner?" Bersk asked.

Reynolds turned back, surprised. "How did you know?"

"Just a lucky guess," Bersk replied.

Tam glanced to his comrade as if to ask the obvious question, and the sellsword replied with a nod.

Another few steps and they heard whispers and mulling about the crowd. When they rounded the corner, the crowd grew silent, and all eyes turned toward the three of them.

"What's the meaning of this?" Reynolds asked. "Clinton, I demand you answer me."

A tan and wiry man at the front of the crowd stepped forward, the hard lines of his face turned in a sneer. "The hunter's fit to be hanged today. Don't see no point in postponing the matter."

"That's not your decision to make."

"Why not, Reynolds? Seems that you're the only one who wants the hunter alive. The hunter's been communing with spirits. Spirits that took the boy. You saw what they did to him!"

The few rattling pitchforks and grumbling voices that rose were silenced when Reynolds spoke, "Listen here! If it is a spirit, the monster hunter says we might need the master alive to deal with it. Do you understand? There'll be no hanging, not until we're sure this thing is dealt with!"

Even Clinton's grumbling quieted. He glared at the bounty hunter. "Is that true?"

Bersk nodded, staring down the group. The crowd shifted nervously, not quite at ease.

"Consider the brilgura," the bard said, folding his arms across his chest. "It is a demon summoned to the mortal plane for a singular purpose, usually selfish and heinous. It is a foul creature, preferring to reside in moist and inhospitable places such as your swamp over there. Were you to kill its master… You would anger it beyond compare, for you have taken its purpose from this world and its means of return to the demonic realms. And you would also free it from all manner of control. Imagine a rampaging, man-eating bull set loose upon your town.”

Tam trailed off with his grisly exposition, and Reynolds added sternly, “I’ll not have anyone mucking this up and setting loose a beast upon our homes. Not on my home, not on my children. I’ll throttle the one of you that steps in that jailhouse before it’s time.”

Dejection swept over the crowd, casting eyes aside and faces down. Bersk was thankful. When times grew perilous, there were fewer and fewer things that would see men to reason. Children and family did not always work, for they were often the reason that men set to hard ways. So it was with banditry—a mix of men with nothing to lose and men with everything to lose.

Bersk added solemnly, “Lend me your faith, and we shall see this through to the end. Give me two days to right this.”

At the front of the crowd, Clinton nodded. The crowd was already turning to go—thankfully, seeing to reason.

Clinton added, “Mind your sellsword, Reynolds. Their kind looks after one another.”

The three of them waited till the crowd dispersed, each man going toward their own hovel. Tam broke the silence. “Honor among sellswords, that’s a new one.”

Bersk shot him a smirk. “Maybe some of us.”

Reynolds led them to the jailhouse, glancing up to Archimedes on the roof. “They’re speaking about the hunter. She used to be like you until she settled here and took to a simple life… Don’t bode well for her with a raven visiting.”

~ ~ ~

Chapter 4
Two Hunters

ELDER REYNOLDS LED the way inside the jailhouse. Somehow, the building seemed even smaller on the inside. The walls were mortar and clay and covered in lichen spots. There were two barred cells and a small sitting area, just wide enough for the three men to stand abreast. In the corner lay a pile of chain mail armor and muck-covered boots. The lingering smell of sweat, mildew, and shit hung in the jail, for there were only two meager cutaway windows.

There was only one occupant. A gray-haired woman sat cross-legged on the straw-covered floor, hands and feet bound to the bars with shackles and chains.

She glanced upward and sighed. "Someone finally saw to reason… at least with one of them."

Reynolds introduced the sellsword and bard, head bowed slightly. Her name was Idina. "They have some questions for you."

"Very well," Idina mumbled. "Get out, Reynolds." She said the words plainly, but bitterness tinged them.

For a moment, the elder's weight shifted uneasily, but he finally nodded and excused himself. "I'll be outside." To his word, Archimedes saw the elder step to the other side of the street.

After the door shut, Idina slumped back against the wall. She looked upon them with tired, red eyes. Purple bruises peered from beneath the shackles. "Ask away, young sellsword."

Bersk leaned against the wall behind him and crossed his arms. "From one hunter to another, you still have that look about you. Patience, measured strength, resolve… What was your specialty?"

"Tracker, longbow… Dagger. What about you, Kevril Bersk? You've got some flavor about you."

"I was a Knight of the Order."

A flicker of recognition passed across her eyes. "I'd say that we're in good hands, but you said *was*—as in, you're not part of the Order anymore. What's the matter? Did you lose your nerve?"

Tam quipped, "It's complicated." And after he saw the side eye of his comrade, Tam added, "Don't mind me. I'll leave this to the professionals."

Bersk turned back to the old hunter. "It was for personal reasons. I'm every bit the hunter I was then."

"…What's that supposed to mean?"

He waved a dismissive hand. "Nothing, nothing at all. I just wonder how a kid dies in these woods, right next to your house. Most towns would pay handsomely for an accomplished sellsword to retire on their land. How long have you been here, Idina?"

"Some thirty years. Long enough to see the fires of the continent burn as Sircius Everdeath passed by this shit stain of a town."

"Tell me how you really feel."

"I feel betrayed, *podex*," the shackled hunter swore. "Do you know what that's like?"

"Yes, I do," Bersk replied simply, ignoring the curse in the old words. The bard beside him didn't move. Whether that was an answer or respectful silence, Bersk didn't know.

"Comes with the trade, I suppose. I just didn't expect it from common folk." She chuckled. "I think the only reason they didn't hang me yesterday is out of respect for their parents and grandparents that took me in."

"Do you know what happened to the child?"

"The same thing that happened to the chickens and the piglet. Someone in a cloak carried them to the swamp... Fed them to something."

"And you saw this happen?"

"I saw them pass into the swamp."

Bersk and Tam exchanged a worried glance. Bersk said, "This person led the chickens and the pigs past your hut? You didn't stop them?"

Idina shrugged. "The townsfolk worship the old gods. That means they make sacrifices. Need a bigger harvest, slaughter a calf. Need a child, slaughter some chickens. I didn't think anything of it."

"What about the child?" Bersk asked, voice raising.

Idina grew quiet. When she spoke, her voice was a trembling whisper. "I didn't know... I was hunting that morning. I watched them from the tall grass. Saw the figure walking. They held another cloak in their arms. It wasn't until an arm slipped out that I knew what it was."

Beside him, Tam stood straighter at attention.

"…You let him go?" Bersk asked, his own voice shaking.

Idina nodded, quiet tears falling. "I don't expect you to understand."

Bersk knelt close to the bars. "For your sake, you must explain it."

"I was scared!" she gasped. "I was… horrified. I froze. Do you know how many men I've killed, Kevril Bersk? Do you know how many women? How many monsters? How long it's been? I've seen—*gods*—I've seen horrors that made men die of fright. But the kid… I don't know what came over me. By the time I had sense enough to follow, they were gone. I ran to the swamp but they were gone.

"I came out of the swamp and laid on the ground in front of my house. Sobbed myself to sleep. The townsfolk came for me in the morning, grabbed me and threw me in here. I didn't find out about the boy until they told me. Said they found him in the trees."

Bersk waited until she stopped and then waited longer for her to compose herself. "Do you have any idea who the cloaked figure could be?" he asked.

Idina shook her head.

"What of the monster? What's out there?"

Idina met his eyes, staring him down. Measuring his worth or his resolve. "I don't know. I hunt game on the outer rim. I don't go deep into the swamp."

"Give me something. Surely a former sellsword that made it to retirement has more to go on."

They shared a half-hearted smirk, like a smothered flame.

She said, "I've only heard breaking branches. They've gotten louder in recent weeks—not deer. Something else is in the swamp." Her eyes grew wide. "He… He might be feeding it."

"One last thing," Bersk said as he stood. "I need to look around your hut. To be sure."

Idina nodded to her pile of clothes. "Do what you must. The key is in my pocket… Be careful, sellsword. May you never meet your match."

Bersk searched her clothes for the single iron key, then piled her clothes again. He turned to Tam, who was looking thoughtfully through the wall, stroking his beard. "We're done here."

"Knight… Does *He* forgive me?"

Bersk turned back to Idina and shook his head. "I don't know. I don't speak for Him anymore… But for what it's worth, I forgive you." He nodded in respect before turning to the task at hand:

Two days to find two monsters—the creature and the one feeding it.

~

Reynolds was waiting for them outside. He ran a hand over his stubbled hair and walked over sheepishly. "Did she help?"

"She did," Bersk replied. He glanced up and down the small town road and saw that no faces lingered from the doors. Reynolds must have shooed them back inside.

"Enough to clear her name?"

Bersk shrugged. "Not yet. You don't think she did it?"

Reynolds shook his head. "Not after living here for so long. She's a hermit mostly, but every other week, she brings game to share with the village. Comes to market and pays a fair price. She's never done wrong by us… I believe she's innocent."

"I believe her," Bersk replied.

"As do I," Tam added. He was still stroking his beard, mulling over details.

"I'll need to see Idina's hut."

Reynolds replied, "Whatever you need to clear her and be rid of the creature."

Bersk nodded. "One more thing… were all the men in the village present earlier?"

Reynolds closed his eyes in recollection. "All but Sidac and Hardegen."

"I'll need to speak with them too," the sellsword replied.

Tam took subtle interest of this—a fleeting tick that the elder didn't notice.

Reynolds's eyes grew wide. "Do you think they had something to do with it?"

"Just exploring all the options," Bersk replied. "The day is still young. Let's not be hasty."

~

Bersk tried to set Reynolds to ease, but there was only so much that could be done for the man. Either way, a child was already dead and someone in the town was likely to blame—unless there was another hermit living in the swamp that Idina didn't know about. Bersk found that unlikely. A hunter would know.

The sellsword and the bard walked the empty stretch of field between the edge of town and the hunter's dwelling. The swamp lay just behind it, growing large in their vision. Bersk could already feel the menace emanating from it, like a dark fog blanketing the landscape. The musty smell of decay settled across the field in much the same fashion.

When they were far enough away from the town, Tam broke the silence. "Guilty before proven innocent," he mused, "I thought we were past such things."

Bersk half-watched as they walked. Archimedes flew high above, checking the fields and the edge of the swamp.

"You've spent too much time in fine company," the sellsword replied. "Life is slower out here… But parts of it are faster. Justice is one such thing. I'm glad they didn't do anything rash."

"Would you blame them?" the bard asked, voice solemn.

"No. No, I would not. We've all done rash things out of anger. Done even worse things out of fear."

Tam looked off across the horizon. "I suppose it's easy to read about things or hear the ballads. Harder to live them."

Bersk smiled. "Sometimes the songs get things right."

"Any ideas so far?" Tam asked, skillfully changing the subject.

Bersk eyed the thoughtful bard, wondering briefly what he had said… Usually the bard was one for philosophy. But Bersk followed the new conversation, resolving to ask him later."

"Two so far. I fear it is someone in the village pulling the strings of the creature.

"Ah, that's why you asked which men were there. Some of which might have a guilty conscience about lynching an innocent."

Bersk nodded, "Second, I fear that creature is a demon…"

"What is it?" Tam asked, for once turning his gaze toward his comrade.

The sellsword smirked. "I also fear you were right."

"Whatever about?"

"The brilgura. So far all the signs point to it." Bersk counted on ungloved fingers for emphasis. "Swamp, tied to a mortal, eats prey whole, leaves behind clean bones... Only you were wrong to compare it to a bull. It's more like a giant toad, and it's not to be taken lightly.

The bard's eyes were wide. "Have you ever fought a brilgura before?"

"I was there while my seigneur—my master—fought one. That was a long time ago." Bersk turned to his comrade and added, "Don't worry. They say when you've fought one demon you've fought them all."

"But they *don't* say that, Bersk."

The sellsword pretended not to hear.

~

Before they crossed the last hundred feet, Kevril Bersk bid Archimedes land on the roof of Idina's hut. Then the raven peered inside the narrow windows. When Bersk was satisfied that the hut was empty, they crossed the final stretch of field.

Bersk mumbled the old words, "*Deprehendere magicae,*" to better see and feel the presence of magic—any wards, traps, or lingering spells that might be a danger.

Idina hadn't mentioned such things, and so Bersk assumed such wards would be minimal. Likely harmless, made to deter a curious child rather than maim an enemy. Regardless, Bersk hated surprises. He unlocked the wooden door and led Tam inside.

In many ways, the hut was unremarkable—merely a hovel placed too far from town. It appeared to be two rooms: One small sleeping area with a wood stove and cot lined with fur skin blankets. The second room contained a blood stained workbench, a rack of tools and knives for working animals and leather. But that was where the mundane ended.

The outside walls—every inch—were covered in runes and script. Normally, only a trained mage knew enough of the old words to discern the spell, but with his own detection spell, Bersk could at least discern the *purpose* of those littered throughout the house.

The walls were covered with nondetection wards, such that someone could not scry on her from afar. Strengthening wards covered the door, should someone try to break in. The thin windows, cut to mirror arrow-slits in a castle wall, were covered with alarm spells—no doubt alerting Idina to Archimedes' earlier presence when he peered through.

Bersk pulled back the thick fur of the top blanket and found warming and protection spells written on the inside skin. He smirked at the former. Most mages the sellsword met were pretentious, preferring to live lives of luxury in service to lords. Bersk wondered what became of Idina's mage, one that had taken to the hunter's protection and comfort so thoroughly. Were they living in a noble's castle or in their own meager sanctuary?

Then there was the floor—suspiciously empty of script. Nothing but bare wooden planks.

"You're awfully silent, Tam," Bersk said idly.

"Merely watching a master work. Like a painting or a sculptor."

"Are you going to take up monster hunting?" Bersk knelt to the ground and began rapping his knuckles on the planks.

"No, merely finding inspiration wherever it lay," the bard replied. "What… What are you doing? Searching for a hidden compartment?"

"Yes. Stop stroking your beard and start on the other end of the hut."

~

Some minutes passed before they found the compartment a hollow between the cot and the wall—not so much heard as felt through the glove of his right hand. Two planks came away and Bersk found more script written on the underside. There were a mix of scripts. One layer of magic to hide what was stashed beneath the floor, and nondetection magic to hide the first layer of magic.

In the ranks of practitioners of magic, Kevril Bersk thought himself in the middle. He was neither generous nor modest about this placement. His job required a mix of warrior and mage, which meant that he was at the pinnacle of neither. He was, however, well-versed enough in both to recognize incredible talent when he saw it.

Whoever had arranged such runes for Idina's hut lay somewhere toward the top of the rankings for magic adeptness. Layering magic in such a way required immense practice and attention to detail. Whatever mercenary life Idina the Hunter had lived, she had made powerful allies.

So Bersk was not surprised by the quiet crackling of static electricity that sounded behind him, nor by the figure who suddenly appeared next to them.

Poor Tam, however, was. "Oh shit," the bard said, hands up in a sign of surrender.

"I must have missed the teleportation runes under the floor," Bersk said. Slowly, he laid the wood plank to the side and sat back on one knee. The sellsword kept his hands raised and still and turned fully to regard the mage.

A woman stood in the center of the room, hands pointed toward Bersk and Tam. With his magic sight, Bersk saw both hands crackling with powerful evocation magic. She was dressed in an ornate evening gown, the color of milk and honey mixed and garnished with heaps of lace trim. She was elven—denoted partly by her pointed ears and fair skin, and the utter frown of an elf torn away from something far more important.

"Who are you and what have you done with Idina?" she asked sternly. "Do not lie or I shall know."

Bersk nodded—of course a mage like her would know how to detect a lie. "My name is Kevril Bersk. The bard beside you is Tamren Jorbough. We know your friend as Idina. She is currently locked in the town jail. They believe she is responsible for the death of a boy. We are trying to clear her name."

"By rummaging through her things?"

"You put it crassly, but yes. I need to know that the hunter isn't hiding anything."

The mage's face softened, but she kept her hands and her magic leveled at them. "I trust you have found nothing then, and it has concluded satisfactorily."

"I have but one place left to look," Bersk said, pointing to the floorboards.

"You may not look down there."

Bersk stomached his frustration. "I need to look there. You have my word that I will take nothing and I shall forget of this place when we leave town."

The mage considered this, measured the truth of his words, and found them satisfactory. Hands still raised, she said, "Look, but do not remove the blade or the treasure that lie under the floorboards."

Bersk pulled an everlit necklace from under his shirt, then leaned over to peer beneath the floor. "*Luminos*," he commanded and willed the small pendant to fill with light.

Beneath the floorboards was a small cubbyhole, no more than a foot wide and three feet long. A single crimson colored bag lay inside, and without looking inside, Bersk could magically discern there were three scrolls of parchment, a half dozen arrows laced with evocation magic, and a single short sword. Of the three, the sword radiated the brightest. It burned with a deep green, with highlights that forked like lightning or vines... Impressive, but not incriminating.

Bersk ended the light from his necklace, returned the planks, then stood and brushed off his front. "Your friend is clear as far as I'm concerned, and an even more accomplished sellsword than she claimed."

"Why is that?" she asked.

"For one, the sword down there hums with druidic magic. Druids loathe metal weapons, and so far as I thought, they wouldn't enchant a sword or similar metal. I imagine she earned the favor of a druid for such a boon. Second, she has earned your watch, and judging by your skill with wards, this was no meager feat either."

The elf's glare softened and she finally relaxed her arms. Magic smoldered at her fingertips. "Friends look after one another, especially when someone is uninvited in their house."

Tam sighed and leaned against the wall. "You've got it wrong, madam. She bid us to search the premises. To clear her name."

The mage's face twisted in concern as the realization dawned on her. "They're going to hang her, aren't they?"

Bersk nodded. "We've got two days to clear her name, but we won't need that long. Don't suppose you'll be staying to help us?"

The mage glanced between the two men before turning to Bersk. "No," she said plainly. "I've my own matters to attend to. Besides, she seems like she's in the capable hands of at least one monster hunter. Save my friend, and you too shall earn a favor, should you need it."

Bersk waved a dismissive hand. "Scant coin is enough."

"I'm afraid you don't understand," the mage replied, her tone becoming serious. "Though I live among you humans, I still respect *the balance*, as all elves should. A life for a life, insult for insult. A favor for a favor."

"A name for a name."

"Krissys Valdove, lady in waiting to Princess Wysana Evancroff. And I must be going now."

Before Bersk or Tam could reply, the mage waved her hands and mumbled words, then she disappeared in a crackling instant.

Tamren slumped down to the floor. "I nearly died of fright from that bloody elf."

"I saw," Bersk said with a smirk. He offered a hand to the bard, but Tam refused.

"I think I'll stay down here for a moment and compose myself. You know, when a special woman comes into your life, they say you never forget it, but that was a tad much. A lady in waiting, no less!"

"I heard. Stroke your beard for a bit. That always makes you feel better. We've got two stops to make before nightfall."

~ ~ ~

Chapter 5
The Guilty and
the Innocent

THE SELLSWORD AND the bard walked the field back to the town proper. The evening sun bled orange into the sky.

"Is that common, for you sellswords to go such very different ways?" Tam asked. "One to rise to the highest ranks of nobility and the other to retire as a hermit?"

Bersk shrugged. "I can't say I've known too many sellswords that get to retire."

"What about the ones you have known, then?"

Bersk looked off into the distance, across the fields to the endless forests on the horizon, and searched himself for the answer.

"I suppose they would go their separate ways," Bersk finally said. "The bonds that hold a group together like that might only last for a mission or two. Sure, there are threads that bind sellswords together, threads that compel Krissys to ward the home of her former comrade, but those threads only extend so far and for so long. I suspect a great deal of years have passed since Krissys and Idina spoke. Such time makes elves and men into different beings."

"You mean the elves' long lives compared to humans?"

"That can't be denied, but I speak of a deeper truth. It is a truth akin to the changing of seasons—this countryside will not be the same in the coming Winter. Or even deeper time— two sides of a riverbank growing apart as the gulf widens between them. Time weathers all things, including friendship."

"I dare say, you've got a poet in you, Bersk. May we travel together long enough to retire, or for I to see your famous trick."

For a few moments, they shared quiet laughter. When it finally died down, Bersk turned to his friend. "On our earlier walk across this field, we talked about adventures and ballads, about the rashness of folk when they're frightened… and you changed the subject. Did I say something that offended you?"

Tam smiled sheepishly, then clasped his hands behind his back—something he did when he meant to be taken most seriously.

"It was nothing you said, Bersk. I like to think that I would tell you if you ever overstepped your bounds. You were right when you said that *sometimes the songs get things right*. Sometimes. Sometimes, at the best. That's why I tag along—not just to see and to write about all those wondrous things, but to *get it right*." The bit of wistfulness left the bard's lips. "But I fear I don't have the stomach for it. Not for much longer, anyway."

Bersk *thought* he had been ready for any answer, but his stomach turned and he fought to keep his composure. "You're leaving?"

Tam shook his head quickly. "Not now. Not yet. But I've thought about it—I won't lie to you."

"It sounds like you've given it quite some thought," Bersk added meekly.

"Well, yes, I suppose I have."

"Tomorrow, I'm going to the swamp. I think you should stay here in town. And I'm sorry about the old scare with Archimedes."

Tam smirked solemnly. "It's not that, and it's not the brilgura. It's the demon summoning… It's the dead lad, too. It's the lot of it. It would be so much easier to live the life of a bard. To bring song and smile. For the worst thing I experience to be petty theft or a night half-paid."

"That's not who you are, though." Bersk said, a quiet plea in his voice. "Back then, you said just the opposite. You said that you wanted to know the truth, to visit those dark and triumphant places. To live the ballads."

Tam nodded. "Oh, I remember what I said. I will never forget it. And I fear I don't have the stomach for it any longer."

Neither friend looked at each other. They both looked off over the horizon, their paths already threatening to diverge.

"Well," Bersk said, "Like you said, you're still mulling it over. You needn't decide now, or anytime soon, for that matter."

The bard patted him on the shoulder. "Indeed."

"At least your songs have been better for it," Bersk added.

"You think so? I still think they're dreadful," Tam said, tongue in cheek.

"Artists are their own worst critic. Or so I've heard."

As they neared the town, the two men set their sights to the job at hand. And at least a while longer, they walked the same path.

~

The sky had turned a muddled red, and the wind had died down when elder Reynolds led them to the house of Sidac—the first of the two men who were not present during the lynch mob.

As they walked, Bersk whispered the words to recast his magic detection spell. Any magic remnants might lead them to summoning books or bindings.

Sidac's family hovel was to the North side of town. Like many of the others, his family house doubled as his trade workspace. Sidac was the resident baker, and the small home barely contained the smell of fresh baked bread and wood stove. Heat billowed from inside.

The door was already open, so Elder Reynolds knocked on the wall, and introduced the sellsword and bard when Sidac came to the door. He was a thin man, with fleeting smile, and tight, dark curls in his hair. His face and clothes were smeared with flour. Sidac beckoned them inside the house, telling them not to mind the lad working oven bellows. The young man shared his father's light complexion and curls, though his hair was a fiery red. Beside him, the stone oven glowed with heat.

Bersk peered across the room to the quaint sleeping quarters, but found no glowing traces of magic. The sellsword quit concentrating on the spell and let it fade.

"Beautiful hair," Tam said to the lad. "The women I know would positively die for curls such as those, or for the men they're on. Red or black." The boy smirked but didn't reply—content to keep at the bellows.

The four men took seats at the square table that no doubt doubled as a workbench—there was a thick layer of flour that seemed worked into the grooves, save for smeared sections on three of the sides where the men sat.

"The red's from his mother's mother, no doubt," Sidac grumbled. He wiped the flour from his hands thoroughly, then folded the rag up and set it aside. "Now, what can I help you men with?"

Bersk glanced across the two rooms of the hovel, but saw no one else inside. "And where is your wife?"

Sidac looked to the elder first, as if silently asking whether he had to answer. "The missus helps at the Hardegen house. He's got one set of hands over there and needs *two sets* to work the weaving machine. Sven is enough help here. Now, what brought you here? I doubt you were after my life story."

"The town seems set on lynching Idina for the death of that boy," Bersk said. "There was a mob out there that wanted to do it today. Damn near all the men in town… Why weren't you there?"

Sidac glared at Bersk, a flicker of annoyance or something else. "I don't think it's right."

"Why not?"

"Idina didn't do it. The boy could've wandered off for all they know."

Reynolds quipped, "The children know better than—"

"Maybe they do, Reynolds. Maybe they don't. Doesn't much matter what the children know," Sidac spat.

Bersk held up a gloved hand to stay the men. "Do you know what happened to the boy?"

"No and neither do Clinton, Denari, or any of the rest of them. They're angry and they're taking it out on Idina, who don't deserve a lick of it." Sidac leaned back, wiry arms crossed.

"You're right," Bersk said, putting a sensitive finger on the table. "They are scared and scared folk are liable to do terrible things if only because they need to do *something*. Lynching that old woman is better to them than stewing in their own fear. Now, you may not like my being here and I don't much care, Sidac. But I agree with you—Idina had nothing to do with it—and neither you nor I want to see an innocent woman hanged. So, tell me something. Give me *something* to work with."

Sidac wiped a spot of flour from his nose, leaving more white there than before. "I don't know," he finally said. "I don't know. I wish I could help you. But I'm just the baker, and I spend most of my days in here doing my job. Not gallivanting around or sneaking out in the middle of the night. Hard to see people's business that way."

Bersk stared back at the man, measuring him. "Did you go into the swamp to look for the boy?"

Sidac's gaze dropped to the table. "No. I… I'm just a baker."

Bersk waited, and was vaguely aware of Reynolds and Tam glancing his direction, waiting for his next question. But the sellsword knew that sometimes silence was better than a question. Silence between two strangers was unnatural and someone would fill it.

Sidac looked back to the sellsword, a pitiful look on his face. "Is that all, Mr. Bersk? If you don't mind, I'd like to get back to work, instead of being reminded how powerless a man can be."

The sellsword nodded, then waved for Tam and elder Reynolds to follow. Before he walked out the door, Bersk added, "I may call on you tomorrow. We've got two days to clear Idina's name."

If Sidac heard, he gave no indication. He was already back at the oven, checking on the bread, his son silently working the bellows.

~

The three men went outside and breathed deep. The evening air felt chilled, though it only felt that way compared to the stifling air of the baker's hut.

Reynolds led them across town. The town seemed to come alive in the short time they were inside. Children ran through the streets and a young woman leaned against a hut. Her skin was deep tan and cheeks adorned with freckles, and she played what might have been a flute or a recorder. Whichever it was, she played it well for the small crowd of half a dozen gathered around her.

Tam nudged the sellsword. "Would you mind?"

Bersk nodded, then bid Reynolds to stay with him a moment on the street to watch the two musicians.

Tam introduced himself to the small crowd and asked if he could accompany the young musician, who nodded tentatively. The bard swung the lute from his back and took his place beside his partner.

One might think a bard of Tamren Jorbough's skill would intimidate or outshine a small town's humble talent, but in Bersk's eyes, that did a disservice to Tam's true skill—accompaniment. Though Bersk couldn't hear the words, he knew what the bard was saying to the young musician. He would tell her to lead, to play whatever she was comfortable with, and he would match her notes.

It was one thing to memorize a song; it was wholly another to play a song one had never heard before.

On their many evenings, Bersk and Tam had spoken of this at length, and compared learning a song to learning magic. Most mages and most bards could only commit a dozen spells or songs to memory at any one time. Those adept at their craft might hold twenty or thirty at a time. Of course, one could always learn more, but there was a sacrifice—an old spell or song might not be recalled well, eliciting a fizzle from a wand or boos from a crowd.

Accompaniment, Bersk and Tam surmised, was more like abjuration and counterspelling. To counter a spell, one had to both recognize the opponent's spell and know the appropriate counter. Performing alongside another was similar, requiring the partner to know the song and the complementary pairing of notes. As such, counterspelling was among the most difficult magic, and learning it was even more complex.

But Tamren Jorbough could improvise and accompany on the fly, as it were. He could stroll into town, and upon hearing a song for the first time, sit down next to the finest musician there and play a duet with them that would make the audience swoon.

The equivalent skill for a mage would be counterspelling at will—in all Kevril Bersk's travels, all the Archmagi he'd met, not one could boast such talent.

When the pair started playing, a stillness fell over the town. The rustling of work and mumblings of conversation from inside the hovels were forgotten. Doors all along the street opened and occupants peered out to see who was making such captivating music.

No matter what the young musician played, be it steady rhythm or cheerful bridge, Tam followed her expertly, and the young musician's notes grew bolder and quicker for it.

Reynolds was in similar form, mouth slightly agape. Bersk, who had heard a great many songs over the years he'd spent with the bard, found this as beautiful as any other.

Bersk likened it to watching a dance kept in perfect time, one partner never overstepping another. Or the meshed gears of intricate clockwork.

When the song faded and finished, the bard kissed her hand and bid her thanks, and she was all smiles. There was little applause because most were too busy wiping their eyes.

Then the young musician began to play again and some of the magic lingered. She played a new song, one with notes of the duet, yet wholly different. Though some faces disappeared inside their homes again, more joined the crowd and listened to her play.

There was one nuance of Bersk's metaphor—musical accompaniment and abjuration—that did not fit and he did not like: Counterspelling another mage meant to take away from the original spell and leave nothing, while Tam's accompaniment added to the original and left the other musician all the better for it.

That was true magic.

Tam slipped the lute strap over his shoulder and rejoined the two men, ushering them silently toward their last stop of the evening. Reynolds's head tilted as if he wanted to say something, but could not find the words. Tam wore a smile of humble joy and Bersk wore his in appreciation.

And as they walked, Bersk felt a pang of sadness at the thought of his friend giving up a life of wandering, the thought of him settling into a comfortable life in a city. One that would reduce his talent to simple playing and not to the pure skill of accompaniment.

That was why Bersk wandered, why he slept on the road and in stables. Because there were a thousand wonders to be seen. Fleeting magic that once glimpsed would never be seen again.

And over the years, his friend had been the source of quite a few of those wonders.

~

The sun was nearly set when the three reached the home of Hardegen, the weaver. It lay on the far side of the village, near Reynolds's house and the remnants of the burned down noble house. The sound of music grew faint, and Bersk recast his magic detection spell one final time.

Elder Reynolds rapped on the door. Inside, the faint squeaks and taps of a loom ceased, and a lock turned behind the door. Hardegen answered the door and beckoned them in.

Hardegen was a strapping lad for a small town. From the breadth of his shoulders and chiseled jaw, he looked to be a young man in his prime. He wore a close-fitted cap and silk shirt nearly as nice as the bard's.

His hovel was equally well kept. Bundles of cotton and wool lined the walls. The main section kept a small oven and table, which was stacked neatly with weaving tools and finished clothes. A single chair and three stools surrounded it. In the second room, a woman with dark, curly hair sat and worked a loom, spinning bulks of gray threads into sheets of fabric. She glanced at Bersk and smiled softly. No magic lingered in the home.

Bersk had been about to greet the Mrs. Sidac, when she saw elder Reynolds and quickly looked away.

"Please, sit," Hardegen said, gesturing to the three stools around the table. "Elder Reynolds, what can I do for you gentlemen so late in the evening?"

The elder nodded to Bersk, and so Bersk explained that he and the bard were there to collect information and to clear Idina's name.

Hardegen leaned back in his chair and scoffed.

"You think she did it?" Bersk said, propping his elbows on the table.

Hardegen nodded. "They found her in front of the swamp, for Movernus's sake. The boy's body was so close it might as well have been next to her."

"Killed him and picked the bones clean? Really?"

"Yep."

"...How?" Bersk asked.

"Did you see her house? Creepy writing all over the walls. It wouldn't surprise me if we'd found her wearing the boy's skin as clothes."

Bersk threaded his fingers together, clenching them subtly. If there was one thing he despised more than a smug noble, it was a smug commoner. It wasn't a good look for the man.

The bounty hunter sighed and buried his feelings as best he could. Beside him, Reynolds was clenching his jaw, muscles on the side of his head flexed.

Bersk said, "You sound pretty sure of her guilt... So, why weren't you at the jail earlier? Seemed like Clinton gathered damn near all the men in the village."

The creeks of the loom slowed.

"Is that why you're here?" Hardegen scoffed. "Reynolds, don't tell me—you think I had something to do with the boy's death?"

"We're exploring all the options," Reynolds said sternly, folding his arms across his chest.

"I was here, *working*. Where Clinton and those others ought to be. Mrs. Sidac was here too. She'll vouch for me."

"I'm sure of it," elder Reynolds quipped.

Hardegen sat forward and wagged a finger at the elder. "You come into my house, nare accusing me of murder. Go and mourn your witch elsewhere."

Reynolds stood quickly, and Bersk followed, hand across the elder's chest. "Gentlemen," Bersk said, "We're merely making sure justice is carried out. No one wants an innocent lynched. We can all agree to that."

Tam was still sitting, and had merely stopped stroking his beard at the outburst.

Hardegen rose hurriedly and gestured for the door. "Now, if you'll excuse me, we've still got a great lot to get done before the night is through."

Reynolds glared at the weaver and said loudly to Mrs. Sidac, "Good evening, Mrs. Sidac. Don't burn the oil too late and keep your husband and son waiting. I'm sure Hardegen can manage."

The men exited, and Tam rose and followed them out.

Hardegen stopped at the door before closing it. "Goodnight, and may wisdom prevail, that you should find the answer that was right in front of you the whole time." Then the door shut swiftly. The lock followed.

"Some history between you?" Bersk quipped.

Reynolds nodded, his eyes boring holes through the door. "Lad's an ass," he said loudly.

"And a womanizer," Tam added, casually.

The elder nodded. "The whole town knows, but they don't speak a word of it. Just whisper."

Bersk nodded. It was good that the elder already knew. It saved Bersk having to spring the truth on anyone. A man's wife spending all day with another man was suspect enough.

But in Hardegen's tirade, a lock of hair had slipped from beneath his cap. A lock of red hair. That detail had both sealed Bersk's suspicions and his doubts.

The young lad living with Sidac was not his son. He was Hardegen's son.

Jealousy can drive a person to do a great many things. Summoning a demon among them. Now the question was discerning which man had done it.

~ ~ ~

Chapter 6
The Things We Do at Night

ELDER REYNOLDS PUT them up in the stables. It was commonplace for the sellsword and bard, as commoners' houses rarely had spare rooms and towns that small didn't have inns. The stables smelled, but they were warm, and by the time clean hay was piled into bedding, the resulting arrangement was comfortable enough and allowed a vagrant to spread out.

The stables were on the West side, the swamp side, of the town. By the time the stall was ready for them, the moon was high in the night sky. Archimedes perched on the roof and had a wide view of the surrounding fields. Bersk doubted the mysterious cloaked figure would try anything that night, not with a sellsword ready for them. In reality, Bersk's eyes hung heavy, and he was thankful for Archimedes. With his sleepless raven watching, Bersk could both keep watch *and* get some shuteye.

But the bard kept talking.

Both men lay in the far back stall. The bard was reclined on a pile of hay against the back of the stall, hands behind his head, legs crossed and foot bouncing. Bersk lay slumped against the outer wall between Tam and the stall door. His gloved hand lay across his chest—they hay was itchy even through the leather of it.

"So, which man do you think it is? Tam asked.

Bersk shrugged. "Could be either: The husband that wants his wife's lover dead. The lover that wants the husband dead."

"Could be the wife."

"I don't think so," Bersk replied. "She seemed like a woman content with the ruse. And more often than not, it is the man that does the killing in situations like that, not the woman. Though, to your point, women often prefer indirect methods, poison, traps, and the like."

"What about the boy?" Tam asked.

Bersk sighed. "Could be."

"Well, I trust you know more about death and its machinations than I do."

"Well, we all have our skills, don't we?" Bersk muttered rhetorically. Thankfully Tam caught his meaning and the silence drug on. Mercifully, Kevril Bersk drifted off to sleep.

~

Archimedes woke Bersk from sleep. Through the raven's eyes, Bersk saw a cloaked figure running through the field, a pig running beside them.

"Well, I'll be damned," the sellsword muttered as he rolled to his feet, startling the bard in the process.

"What is it?" Tam asked, wide eyed.

"The figure. Be a good man and keep watch from the door. If someone should try to follow me, don't let them. And if you get the time, stop by our two mark's houses and see who isn't home." Bersk was already out the door and running across the field, cloak trailing in the shadows of the field. Archimedes flew across the night sky, following the cloaked figure.

Bersk kept up with the figure, but did not want to catch them. Not yet.

Watching through Archimedes's eyes, the sellsword could keep his steps in time with the figure and knew just when to duck down as they looked nervously over their shoulder.

Twice they stopped and turned, and twice the figure saw nothing but an empty field.

Archimedes slipped through the branches above, following them into the swamp. Just as the water began to get shin deep, stones rose to meet the figure's feet, revealing a path into the swamp.

Kevril Bersk followed a hundred paces behind. He steeled himself against the smell and ducked under vines to enter the swamp proper. Thankfully, the stones of the secret path stayed where they were and allowed him to follow without wading through the murky water.

The figure led the pig a few hundred paces more, and as they walked, the pig grew less and less docile, its squeals growing from muted protests to struggle. They dragged the pig the last fifty feet before stopping at a small pond. Skeletons were all around, tangled in the vines above. Through Archimedes's eyes, Bersk saw small rodents, birds, half a dozen pigs and one boy—all pristine white.

Kevril crept closer, muttering a spell of silence to aid his steps across the stones. When he was one hundred feet away, he stepped carefully off the path and dispersed the spell. From there, he saw the figure and the pig both through his own eyes and through Archimedes's, and he could hear the mutterings through the raven.

"I return to you with another offering, Orrek-Nul," the man said, waving his arms in a wide, invocative gesture. "Please accept this flesh, I give to you."

Bubbles rose in the green muck. They burst and receded slowly after. As seconds passed, the bubbling grew to a boil and a massive dome crested the surface—fifteen feet wide. The pond receded as the massive bulk of the brilgura rose. Its skin was a deep brown, saggy and thick, its wide white eyes peering from behind thick folds. Its back limbs were tree-trunk thick and rippling with otherworldly strength. Sickly curved claws tipped the forelimbs and back legs, and spines protruded from the joints and through folds of skin, seemingly at random.

The creature spoke, its lips barely parting, yet the bellowing voice sent ripples across the vines and water. Its voice was deep and underlaid with scraping brimstone. The rotten egg smell of sulfur overwhelmed the swamp.

"This is not what I asked for!"

"I—I know," the cloaked man stuttered, hands raised in front of him in pitiful defense. "I could not bring a child."

The great mouth parted, revealing thousands of needle thin teeth, and a bright pink tongue shot out. The thick flesh was across the pond and coiled around the head of the pig in a single instant. The muffled cries were short, for the brilgura retracted its tongue with the same viciousness, dragged the pig limply across the muck, and swallowed it whole.

When the creature spoke again, its voice was just above a whisper—so quiet that Bersk could only hear through Archimedes.

"*Bring me a child. Bring me Fara.*"

"No—please, no."

"*We had a deal.*"

"But I didn't know. I just wanted him gone... I didn't know others would have to die."

"*And do you remember what happens if you don't keep your word?*" The creature's mouth parted enough to reveal slivers of teeth and four swirling tongues. From somewhere inside, agony-filled squeals could barely be heard.

The cloaked man nodded.

"*Bring me the child Fara. Now!*" the brilgura hissed.

"Y—Yes, Orrek-Nul."

The cloaked man turned and walked back the way he came. From Bersk's hiding spot, he could just make out through the vines the silhouette of the man and monstrous demon lurking behind him.

"*Wait,*" the demon breathed. The man froze, shaking in fear beneath his cloak. "*...There is someone here.*"

The brilgura hissed rhythmically, chanting in demonic tongue, and the entire swamp began to writhe. Sulfur hung heavy in the air. The water around Berk's feet ebbed and churned as if it were alive—then something forceful brushed his boot. A slithering face broke the surface, stared at the bounty hunter, then disappeared. Then another—then another.

Tadpoles churned around his ankles and more converged on him from all around. Their bodies covered in thick, viscous slime.

"*There you are,*" the brilgura whispered.

Before Bersk could run or look, the coiled tongue wrapped around his torso like a bola, and yanked him toward the pond. Toward the waiting maw of the brilgura.

Bersk had just enough time to summon his magic sword and slash through the thick tongue. He slumped to the ground, threw the limp coil of flesh off him and rose to face the brilgura—standing much, much closer than he had moments before. The frog demon seemed like a living wall in front of him.

Somewhere behind him, the cloaked man was sprinting out of the swamp. With any luck, Tam or some of the others from town will have them in custody before long.

"How dare you come into my *swamp!"* The demon bellowed spittle and bile through the air, of which Bersk turned sideways to dodge two larger chunks.

"You're no longer welcome here, demon." Bersk replied defiantly. He held *Twitch* in his right hand, left hand with a loose grip, the stance of a Knight. Moonlight glistened off the gruesome blue curves of the blade.

Four coils of tongue sprung forth to catch the sellsword, and Bersk lopped off each one with neat flicks of his wrist.

The brilgura growled, shaking the entire swamp.

Without the cloaked figure here, there was no hope of killing or banishing the demon. Bersk needed to escape back to town and drag the summoner back to the swamp.

It was a good thing that demons could feel pain.

The sellsword bid Archimedes to change.

The raven fell from the branches and into the muck—so small that the demon didn't notice it. But moments later, Archimedes rose out of the water, hairless, bone white face, massive shoulders of an Ugu. Though the brilgura was bigger, Archimedes stood face to face with it.

Something akin to shock passed over the brilgura's face as it turned to face an equal creature.

Kevril Bersk commanded two more things of Archimedes: *Thrash it. Return when it retreats.*

The Ugu howled and slammed its fists down on the brilgura. Impacts echoed through the swamp, each like a tree slamming into the ground. It pummeled the demon, over and over, like titanic drum beats—each vibrating through the soft ground. The beast's arms became a whirl of rust-colored fur. It smiled with its huge tusks and grunts akin to laughter sounded over the maelstrom.

For a moment, the brilgura was cowering and overshadowed. Then it pounced.

The demon screamed and leapt with frightening force, slamming head-first into the Ugu, and careening across the swamp. Vines, branches and whole trees broke beneath the titanic creatures. They sailed some thirty feet past Bersk and crashed into the muck, threw up waves of water and felled trees in their wake.

"*Aqua deambulatio,*" Bersk said. The magic words raised him up to the surface of the addled water and the sellsword ran across it, muck rippling beneath his steps and leaping over the waves.

The Ugu howled and struggled beneath the bulk of the frog demon; the brilgura pushing the beast down into the muck.

The sellsword was upon them in a breath.

The brilgura sensed his approach and kicked back with a single hind leg. Bersk slipped to the right side of the demon, the giant leg passing close enough that he felt the breeze. He slashed with *Twitch* across the back of the demon's outstretched leg, severing the powerful tendon and jarring against the bone. Three more times, *Twitch* flashed across the monstrous back leg to be sure it was rendered useless.

It turned to face the sellsword, snarling. Half a dozen tongues shot out like spears toward Bersk, and he sliced through each with a flash of the shimmering blade.

The demon's mouth opened wide, revealing the countless rows of needle teeth and tongues, the skin inside of the mouth appearing to boil. Bersk readied himself for the creature's pounce—he would have one chance to duck, to slip beneath it and rend it from beneath.

But to his surprise the demon turned round, bellowing in agony. As it turned, The Ugu was holding onto its wounded leg, arms wrapped around the demon's upper thigh, sinking its teeth and tusks into the frog's leg. Black blood sprayed, and the brilgura whipped around in a lurching frenzy, unable to turn its mouth enough to bite or reach back far enough with its forelimbs to scrape away its attacker. The swamp quaked beneath their feet.

Bersk spun twitch in front of him, the tip of the blade making a ritual circle between him and his target. The sellsword uttered the words, "*Mora ordinem*," the spell of *Lingering Balance*, and the old druid words, "*Astar na gaoithe*," the *Speed of the Wind*.

To concentrate on multiple spells was among the greatest skills a Magi or Knight could learn, but there were other ways. Bersk's goddess of Order empowered the sword—freeing the humble sellsword from keeping up the spell. The *Water Walk* spell was already fading and in a few moments, Bersk's feet would sink into the muck again.

But Bersk only needed a moment. *Twitch* glowed with divine power. Blue ether dripped from the blade.

As the two giant monsters spun in their frenzy, the Ugu holding onto the wounded back leg of the brilgura, Bersk dashed through the stampede, slipping around the brilgura like the wind, and slashing thrice at each unmarred leg, all before the brilgura had spun around a single time.

The sellsword stepped away, and the stampede slowed. The brilgura's body collapsed to the ground, wounded legs unable to support its bulk. Blue dripped from the wounds. Still, the demon struggled.

In desperation, the brilgura rolled over on its back, then around completely. It tumbled across the swamp, snapping trees, and smashing the Ugu beneath its massive body.

The Ugu lost its grip and fell off, and the brilgura hissed and turned from the hunters. The demon crawled and lurched through the swamp, retreating.

"Run, Orrek-Null!" the bounty hunter shouted in between breaths.

Archimedes was already shrinking, changing back to its raven form. The bird flitted over to Bersk's shoulder. Breathing heavy, he bid Archimedes follow the brilgura again from the tops of the trees.

The raven flew away to follow the demon, and the bounty hunter willed his sword away. He cast *Water Walk* again and ran over the muck back to the village.

~ ~ ~

TAM WAITED—FOR how long, he couldn't say, but long enough that Bersk had crossed the woods and disappeared into the swamp. Then he adjusted his shirt and walked as nonchalantly as he could across the quiet town in the dead of night.

Tam was used to the cities. They were always alive with people, with movement and light. It seemed like there were two bloody torches in all of Keld.

Hardegen's house was closest, and soon Tam was standing in front of it.

Normally, he would've looked through a window, but these quaint dwellings had only meager slots to let light in. Most were covered with taut animal skins to keep out the worst of the elements. Instead, the bard walked around the side of the house, listening for any sign of life inside. Thankfully, it didn't take long.

There was a rustling inside, and Tam pressed his ear to the wall. A woman moaned quietly, then a man a moment later. Tam's cheeks flushed and he pulled away.

So much for Hardegen being the culprit.

He turned to leave and froze—

In a narrow alley across the street, there was the unmistakable silhouette of head and shoulders. Someone was watching him. Something glinted in the moonlight—a blade.

Tam swallowed and walked quickly around the back of the house. He stopped in the darkness and listened.

Footsteps. Coming in his direction.

"Godsdamnit," the bard whispered. He clutched the knife tucked in his vest pocket.

It could've been nothing. Could've been just a concerned citizen. *Or it could be an accomplice.* Tam's mind went back to the knife glinting in the moonlight.

His own knife was a meager comfort. Tam supposed he could always scream.

Tam walked quickly around the back of another house, walking closer to the center of the village. Then he walked between two houses, back to the mainstreet.

And ran straight into Clinton.

Clinton took a swig from the bottle in his hand, then wiped his chin with his forearm.

Clinton staggered forward. Tam unconsciously took a step back into the alley. It took a moment to realize that the glint in the moonlight had been the bottle. When he realized this, the bard stood up straight, tried to stand his ground, but Clinton was a full head taller than him and reeked of booze. Tam kept a hand on his vest pocket.

Clinton's face turned into a sneer. "You want a go with her?"

It took a moment to register what he said. Tam shook his head. "You've got me figured wrong, good sir."

Clinton lurched a step forward, then leaned in close. The smell of booze made Tam wince.

"I saw you playing your lute with little Lucille. Maybe you like 'em young."

There were times in his life that Tamren Jorbough wished he was a bigger man, or that he was skilled with a blade. This was one of those times.

Tam said again, "You've got me figured wrong. I prefer theatrical women. They're—how should we say—more *lively*."

Clinton frowned. "You think you're better than us. Know better than us. Well, you're wrong." He leaned forward again, painfully close to the bard. "And your sellsword friend isn't here to say different."

Tam bit back the obvious insult, *better than you*. It was never smart to antagonize a drunk, nor a man bigger than oneself.

There were also times in his life that Tam wished he could let things go.

Tam said, "How about you, old boy? Do you fancy the sheep or the goats?"

Clinton clocked him in the head.

Tam was thrown sideways and slumped against the wall of a nearby house. His head swam, ears rang. It wasn't the worst shot he'd taken—there had been many over the bard's long career from angry drunks and angry husbands. Of course, usually he was smart enough to piss off a noble and not someone who clearly worked with their hands.

Clinton growled and dropped the bottle. Then he grabbed Tam by the shirt, and picked up Tamren like he was a sack of flour—held him against the wall.

The drunk sneered, "You'll pay for that."

Tam held up a shaky hand to stay him. "Alright, alright. Point taken... Pigs it is."

The bard almost laughed—not at his own joke—at how wide Clinton's eyes went. The next painful seconds were almost worth it.

Almost.

Clinton punched Tam in the stomach, knocking the wind from him and doubling him over. Then Clinton shoved him back up against the wall, ready to hit Tam again—

Tam winched and braced himself for a punch that never came.

"Who is..." Clinton whispered, then shouted, "That's them!"

Clinton ran, and without his support, Tam collapsed to his knees on the dirt. He coughed and wheezed to catch his breath.

Tam had to give it to him, the pig-lover could hit.

The bard picked himself up, vaguely aware of more shouting from the fields. *Shit*, he thought, *there could only be one them in the field at this hour*. Tam found his feet and shuffled out of the alley, picking up speed into the tall grass.

In the distance, Clinton was cursing and pummeling someone else.

"Help!" Tam shouted weakly. He sucked air and tried again. "Help, anyone! Everyone!"

Clinton held onto the man's cloak and swung wildly with his other hand, causing them both to spin in a drunken waltz.

"It's Sidac!" Clinton screamed.

Tam was nearly upon them, his head just then feeling like it was screwed on straight, when he was shoved aside by someone else. They too set upon Sidac, wrestling to hold him.

Whatever vengeance and fury Sidac had coming to him, Bersk would need him alive.

"That's enough!" Tam shouted. He strode over and shoved Clinton as hard as he could, sending the unexpecting drunk sprawling across the ground. He turned to the other figure— Hardegen—and said forcefully, "We need him."

Hardegen didn't turn or stop, and a moment later, Tam was shoved and fell hard to the ground—Clinton was already up and grasping for Sidac.

Tam struggled to his feet, hearing panicked steps and shouting of more villagers. Someone that might've been Elder Reynold's yelled for Idina.

The field became a blur. Men had brought clubs. It seemed half wanted Sidac to answer for his crimes, and the other half wanted him dead right there in the field. As the struggle ensued, it felt very much to Tam that more of the village was in the second latter half.

~ ~ ~

Chapter 7
The End of suffering

KEVRIL BERSK EMERGED from the swamp, limbs filled with the dull burn of exertion, and came face to face with a mob. Hoisted torches and shouts and screams overshadowed the moonlight.

And in the center, someone was being beaten.

The sellsword called on his minor magic, amplifying his voice a dozen times. "*Halt!*" he bellowed, his voice sending ripples across the field.

The crowd turned and cowered, like rabbits before a fox. Tam was the first to step forward. "Bersk! You must stop them." The right side of his face was gashed and his lip wept blood down his beard, but he stood steadfast.

Anger seized Bersk's chest and he strode forward. Anger must have seeped across his face and his gate, for the whole of the village parted without words.

In the center, Bersk found half a dozen men surrounding the cloaked man. His hood had fallen back, revealing Sidac, the baker. He lay crumpled on the ground, face beaten to a reddened pulp. Hands shaking.

His wife pushed her way through the men and knelt on the ground with him, cradling his head.

Clinton and Hardegen stood at the front of the group—Bersk recognized the other four from the earlier lynch mob. The men held clubs and hammers, tools of their trades turned from humble purpose.

Elder Reynolds and Idina the hunter stood to the side with the rest of the townsfolk. Bersk saw them plainly, now; many were nursing injury already, those two included. Idina held a knife tucked in front of her.

"We've got this under control, sellsword," Hardegen said. "There's no innocents here."

"I'm sure of that," Bersk sneered. "There's just one problem, gentlemen. The brilgura is still in the swamp. I need Sidac to banish it, and I need him able to speak."

"Use your *magic*," Clinton said, enunciating the last word. "We'll deal with the demon worshiper." Clinton turned back toward Sidac, eliciting groans from both man and wife.

The sellsword held out his gloved right hand and *Twitch* appeared. Gasps echoed through the crowd as they backed away, leaving just the defiant men and Kevril Bersk in the middle of the field. Clinton, Hardegen, and their men turned toward the sellsword and raised their weapons hesitantly.

Bersk said, loud enough for all to hear, "Clinton, what the bard told you in front of the jail is true: You kill the summoner and you'll loose the demon upon your village. What's more, either of you touch him again and I will do worse to you than the demon. Think of your village and, if you can't do that, think of yourselves."

Silence hung in the air, punctuated by Sidac's labored breathing.

Slowly, sense came to the men and they lowered their weapons. Bersk gestured with his sword for them to back away, then he and Tam went to Sidac's side. His wife wept quietly and clutched her husband's hand.

Bersk turned to the bard. "Can you help him?"

Tam nodded, unperturbed by his own injuries. "*Sana vulnera suum.*" Tam waved his hand over the bruised face and moments later, the blood slowed and some bruises receded. "That should help."

Behind them, elder Reynolds was bidding everyone to return to their homes.

Idina stooped beside them. "Will he live?"

Tam nodded. "His wounds look worse than they are."

"I tried," Idina said, clearly frustrated. "By the time Reynolds let me out…"

"It is past us," Bersk said, putting a hand on the hunter's shoulder—in the moment, he had mistakenly used his gloved hand. He removed it nearly as quick. The sensitivity made touching someone—even shaking hands with it—far too intimate to be comfortable. All at once through the glove he had felt the tautness of her shoulder muscles, even the warmth of her skin. He cast his eyes down to hide any reaction.

When the swelling had gone down enough for Sidac to speak, the poor man grasped the arm of his wife and mumbled, "I'm sorry. I'm sorry. I'm sorry." Mrs. Sidac said nothing, just ran her fingers through his hair.

Bersk stood and pulled the bard to his feet, then brushed off the bard's shirt and straightened out his sash. "There you go, Tam. Good as new." Though he tried to jest, Bersk's stomach turned at the sight of his friend besmudged.

The bard thumbed his busted lip and smirked. "I think you missed a spot."

"Your enduring fans will see to that."

Tam chuckled. "I've had enough of my fans for the evening. Thank you kindly. I seem to recall that someone said I would be safe in town."

"This is the field."

Tam gestured to his face, "I got all this before this field nonsense."

Bersk glanced away from his friend, dejection and frustration swirling in his gut. "I'm sorry, Tam."

"Think nothing of it. It's a flesh wound. Good for the lyrics."

The sellsword frowned. "Not for that... I need your help. I need you to come with me to make sure our summoner doesn't run away while I'm dealing with the brilgura."

"Oh…" Tam said, bewildered. "Isn't that what Archimedes is for?"

Bersk shrugged. "Archimedes is following the demon to its lair. I fear it's already helped me enough for the day. Even the psychopomp has its limits."

From the ground, Sidac mumbled, "I'll go. I won't run away."

"I know you won't," Bersk replied. "That's why my friend didn't heal you completely."

"I'll go," Tam said, eyes unflinching.

"I'll go too," Idina said with a resolve of steel. "I'll get my bow."

Before either of them could reconsider, Bersk stooped down to the ragged man and the distraught wife. "Mrs. Sidac,

I need you to help him up. The bard and I will see him the rest of the way."

She looked up with red, wet eyes. She asked through clenched teeth, "Please, bring him back to me."

In spite of his vow, Kevril Bersk found himself judging Mrs. Sidac, wondering if her sadness was guilt, anger, fear, or promise of recompense… or perhaps a mix of all. Not that it mattered.

"Ma'am, I will see your husband through the swamp, to the nest of the demon. Together, we will banish it and you and the town will never trouble over it again. Then, and only then, will I bring your husband back to you."

To be a Knight or a hunter was to walk a perilous path. It was not noble, as it was to be a soldier or a priest. It was fraught with the tattered banner of humanity, set upon all sides by pain and loss and grief. Many times, the Knight was the cause of such suffering, and it was a weight that most could not bear for long.

So, when Bersk lied to Mrs. Sidac, it was not to spare her from suffering. It was to spare himself.

~

Elder Reynolds had spurred the rest of the village back to safety, though Bersk doubted any of them would sleep that night. To their credit, some of the men of the former mob offered to come into the forest; they had stood defiantly enough when offering their service, but Bersk could see the subtle fear in the men's eyes—something he might've missed had he not seen Idina's resolve moments before.

Kevril Bersk took only Idina, Tam, and pitiful Sidac into the swamp with him.

From high above, the raven watched the demon. Through Archimedes's eyes, Bersk saw the brilgura prostrate and writhing before its twisted, towering altar. Bersk would not let Archimedes get closer, for the demon was gravely wounded and liable to lash out at anything that caught its attention.

Archimedes couldn't die—not in such a crude sense—but the psychopomp could feel pain; Bersk strove to keep that to a minimum.

The group walked the hidden stone path into the swamp. Bersk stayed half a dozen steps out front. Sidac limped behind and leaned on Tam for support. Idina stalked an equal measure behind them, bow at the ready. Periodically, Sidac mumbled in demon tongue to conjure the next segments of the stone path.

It would've been quicker to cast *Water Walk* on the lot of them, but that would spread the magic thin, and Bersk needed to save his power for the brilgura. Archimedes had been kind enough to take the brunt of the demon's first onslaught. Now that challenge would fall to Bersk.

"Why'd you do it?" Idina whispered, breaking the tense silence.

Bersk glanced back and found Sidac looking off to the side, hiding his eyes from the others.

"I hate him," Sidac mumbled. "I hate him so much. He's taken my wife from me… I thought that after our son was born, it would be different. And it was, for a while. Every time I caught her glancing at Hardegen at market or during service, I told myself there was no harm in it. No harm in a look. When our son was five, she said he was old enough to help me. She said Hardegen needed help—"

"I don't want to hear it," Idina hissed. "Why Sven? Why the boy? What did he do to deserve being eaten?"

Sidac's breath quivered. "Not a thing. Not a damn thing."

Bersk said, "Sidac conjured the brilgura to take care of Hardegen. But demons demand sacrifice. He didn't know what it would ask for."

"At first it demanded prayers," Sidac said. "Just prayers, every night for a year. That's what the book said, but then I heard its voice. It called me to the swamp. It was just a tadpole... but gods, its voice! It asked for mice. Then chickens, the pigs. Then it asked for Sven—*by name*. I... I... If I didn't, I knew it would be me instead."

Idina said, "It should've been—"

"That's enough," Bersk said quietly. The sellsword turned. "Look at me, Sidac. A demon won't harm its master. I tell you this, not to shame you, but to prepare you. We are going to the brilgura's lair and we are going to banish it. Only *you* can do that. You need to utter the summoning spell again—do you remember it?"

Sidac nodded, eyes wide and bloodshot.

"Good," the sellsword replied. "Now, it won't take kindly to that, but you just keep mumbling the words. I'll take care of the brilgura."

"*We*," Idina corrected. "I may not be getting paid for this, but this is my village."

Bersk cracked a smile. "I trust you. I'll take care of the brilgura. You take care of me. Tam takes care of all of us. We'll all earn our keep tonight. Now Sidac, where's this book?"

~

Sidac led them across a fork in the walking path. Unlike the other paths that rose tens of feet in front of them as they walked, this path stayed hidden until Sidac was directly over top of it. The injured baker waved for them to stay back, and mumbled demonic words and walked to their timing. Stone steps rose up to meet his feet and then a pedestal rose up in front of him. It was simple in design, made of weathered stone, and just wide enough to hold a single book—unmarked and bound in black leather. Despite its coming from the ground, the pages and binding were dry and free of mud and dust.

Bersk stood on the main path, a few paces behind Sidac. "Now give me the book," Bersk said.

Sidac picked up the tome and ran his hands over the face of it. "My grandmother found this some decades ago. Handed down some of the secrets to my ma, and then she to me. She told me never to use the spells for more than the smallest of things: A good harvest, a little rain here or a little sun there. Truth be, I don't think the town ever noticed." Sidac nodded. "That's the way she wanted it. That's the way it should've been…"

Idina moved to step forward, but Bersk held out a hand to stay her.

Sidac looked to the waiting group, his eyes growing stern. "Do you know the first time I used it? *Twenty years ago.* We saw black smoke on the horizon, so much that the sun could scarcely rise. We… We didn't know what it was at first. I just knew that I had to use the book. I asked whatever gods or demons were listening to spare our village. And they did. No one in town never questioned why we survived Everdeath's crusade when half the continent didn't. They said we were too small to be noticed.

"I never told a soul," Sidac continued, squeezing the book, arms quaking. "And what thanks did I get? My wife looking elsewhere. I didn't call on the brilgura those first months before our son was born. I didn't call on it when he was five and she went back to Hardegen. Years I waited… Years…"

When Sidac trailed off, Bersk stepped forward smoothly and took the book from the baker's hands. Sidac let it go.

"I'll hang onto that for now." Bersk pocketed the book and put his left hand on the man's shoulder, though Sidac wouldn't meet his eyes. "We can never erase the things we've done. Not ever. But see this through. If nothing else, it is a start."

Sidac glanced meekly to the others and then back to Bersk. "I'm ready."

~

They walked deeper and deeper into the swamp, following the hidden stone trail. The howls of the brilgura were close now and the ground shook softly from its writhing.

Bersk willed Twitch to his hand and the blade appeared silently from the ether. He crouched low and waved the others to him. Their faces were weary. Tam and Sidac shrank from the echoing growls as they ebbed over the swamp. Idina didn't flinch, but she stared wide-eyed in the direction of the brilgura—her gaze never once faltering from that direction.

"Things are going to happen fast," Bersk whispered. He looked to Tam. "Take care of yourself and Idina."

Tam furrowed his brow. "What about you? Won't you need warding?"

"No," Bersk replied. "I have a few tricks left."

Sidac nodded. "And the brilgura won't hurt me, right?"

"Right you are, Sidac," Bersk replied. "Keep your eyes open, though. It's going to be angrier than you can imagine and thrashing about like a wild… well, like a crazed demon. So, don't get hit by an errant flailing of its limbs."

Bersk glanced to the rest of them. "I'm going to rush in and draw it away. Then Sidac can run to the shrine and start the banishing prayers. Idina, then you can engage. After that, it's all a matter of how fast we can wound it and how fast Sidac can banish it."

Then the bounty hunter turned round and ran toward the profane altar. Through Archimedes's eyes, he saw the writhing demon and then the rustling foliage that marked his own approach. Seeing these things from afar in no way prepared Kevril Bersk for what he saw. He ran through the trees that lined the clearing, then stopped in his tracks.

The brilgura writhed on the ground, rolling and twisting, limbs jerking. The spines that stuck out from its body were softening, bending like saplings. Its cries grew in pitch to squeals.

Great spikes shot up from the ground, piercing the brilgura as it writhed, then retracted into the ground. It was as if the frog demon were rolling on a bed of nails. Blood splashed the dirt and pooled on top of it like spilled paint.

The jagged altar behind the demon rose up three stories in the air, made of twisting bramble and bone white stone. The pooled blood on the ground was rolling and seeping toward the base of the altar turning the pale structure shades of pink and red.

From the edges of the clearing, tadpoles pushed through the treeline, climbing over top of one another. Their heads dried, cracking. Desperate voices bubbled from them.

"Help us." "Kill us." "She's sucking us dry." "Why, why, why."

Bersk's eyes grew wide. Until that moment, he'd thought that the brilgura was merely recuperating...

But the brilgura was beseeching its mother, Ariazi—mother of all demons—for aid. The frog demon was sacrificing its own blood and offspring for power. Not unheard of, but it would complicate things considerably. And Bersk regretted not saving Archimedes's talents for the engagement.

The bounty hunter waved his left hand in the sigil of frost and spoke the words, "Primum terram gelu." The ground beneath the demon hardened and turned to ice, slowly and finally stopping the spikes from beneath the ground—halting the demon's sacrifice.

The brilgura rolled over in a frenzy, digging its strong claws into the ice for traction. It turned and glared at Bersk. "*Little hunter here to test his luck again. I knew you'd come. You're too late. Mother has blessed me. She deemed your death worthy.*"

The altar began to whine like a finger upon a wet glass. The noise grew to a pulse, like a beating heart. Great cracks split the length of the altar and stone fell away in slivers, revealing a veiny flesh beneath.

The ice below the demon melted, the magic of the spell pushed back by the strength of the demonic altar.

Then the brilgura began to change. Its already formidable bulk grew larger, the thick muscles swelling and bulging until it looked like the skin might burst. The flaccid spines stretched and turned to lashing whips, their tips fraying and turning into braided flails. Tongues stretched from its mouth and teeth filled the spaces between.

"*Stercus,*" the bounty hunter cursed.

Bersk traced the sigil for an arcane blast, then pointed with his sword. Pure arcane power shot forth, and careened into the brilgura. Ripples of impact washed over the swamp and Kevril Bersk took off running, skirting to the left and around the creature.

The mutated frog demon turned and lashed out with tendrils and tongues. Bersk twisted and slashed with his sword, skirting some and lopping off others. The detached sections slithered idly on the ground.

"You're going to have to do better than that," Bersk teased, leveling *Twitch* at the creature.

The brilgura bellowed, deep and menacing, and then charged. Its crazed bulk had given it a lumbering gate, so big it could no longer jump. So heavy the ground rattled with each step.

"*Fìonag dealanaich*," Bersk said as he signed and touched the sword to the dirt. *Twitch* crackled with lightning. Bolts leapt from the sword and dove into the ground. The ground between man and demon smoldered with power, then the bolts shot up through the charging demon with thundercracks.

As Bersk suspected, the bolts only served to anger the charging beast. Anything to take its attention away from the altar.

Through Archimedes's eyes, Bersk saw Sidac already kneeling before the altar, hands waving and muttering the banishing incantations. To Bersk's right, flashes of Idina and Tam were just visible through the trees. They were flanking the beast.

"*Vires et voluntatem*," Bersk whispered. Strength flowed into his muscles and his chest swelled with confidence. The bounty hunter stared down the stampeding, overpowered demon, and charged right at it.

As the bounty hunter charged, three arrows whizzed through the air and pierced the side of the brilgura. Fire sparked from the wounds, but the demon didn't stop or flinch. When they were upon each other, the brilgura opened its mouth wide. A thousand teeth flashed at Kevril Bersk, but not one eye—the brilgura had relinquished them for power.

The bounty hunter leaned back and slid beneath the monster, his face a half foot away from its underside. Twitch slashed seven times across its vulnerable belly before momentum carried Bersk to the other side. Blood sloshed from beneath the beast.

The brilgura careened over him, slashing at the ground for traction and finding none. The brilgura crashed into the treeline, shaking the ground with its thrashes and bellows.

Four more arrows sailed across the scene and stuck into the monster. Between the hunter's skill and the bard's blessings, each found their mark.

Bersk rose and sprinted after the creature, desperate to keep its attention.

"*Mora ordinem*," Bersk said, flashing the ritual circle with his sword. He descended on the demon with a flurry of his magic sword. The brilgura had not yet righted itself and was seeping from a half dozen more wounds—each bleeding blue.

It lashed out with tentacles and its giant back legs, and Bersk rended each of them with *Twitch*. Bersk whipped around the brilgura, suddenly aware that more and more arrows were sticking out of its hide—so long as they didn't pull the demon's gaze back to the altar.

Then the brilgura's back legs split and writhe, each leg severing into a dozen more flail-studded tendrils. Each whipped at the bounty hunter with discordant frenzy.

Two lashed Bersk across his shoulders and another across his thigh. A single impact would've shattered bones and felled a normal man, but between Bersk's armor and bolstering spell, he stood fast, sword flashing.

"*Astar na gaoithe*," Bersk said, tracing another sigil. In the half-second it took to cast the *Speed of the Wind*, Bersk was lashed twice more. Warm blood dripped down his sleeve and down his sword hand.

Again, Kevril Bersk was a blur, his speed elevated above that of mere mortals. *Twitch* moved in flashes and the world seemed to slow down, as if everyone but him were moving underwater.

Limb after limb reached for Bersk, and each was cut down. Beneath his feet, felled slivers were seeping into the ground. To his left, arrows were drifting across the clearing. Through Archimedes's eyes, he saw Sidac rising, arms wide and shouting profane words—finishing the banishment spell.

Sidac was close enough done with the spell that the brilgura was turning toward the altar, sensing its immediate end.

Tendrils lashed out, extending toward the altar and toward Sidac. Bersk cut them all down.

The profane altar began to quake. Sidac's voice rose to a crescendo. The end was near.

The brilgura's voice slowed to a rumble as it called out, "*Ariazi, my flesh, my life, my name for your glory.*"

Then the demon shuddered and then its body split along three lines. What moments before had been ribs and organs and tendons, rose out of the back of the brilgura—extending, lengthening, the tips becoming spined and sickly. The brilgura bloomed like an unholy forest.

Bersk ran between the monstrosity and the altar. So far, he'd been milking his magic, and the time for subtlety was gone.

"Tam! Are you watching closely?" Bersk called.

As the unholy blossom of tentacles turned toward the bounty hunter, Bersk whispered and signed, "*Vetiti ordinis: Ororrim effigies.*" One of his goddess's forbidden spells—one of his personal favorites.

The man that was Kevril Bersk became many. Copies of himself appeared from the ether. Ten, to be exact. All wearing the same enchanted armor and wielding *Twitch*.

A storm of tendrils descended on Bersk's squad of duplicates, and they were met with a dam of blades. Ten flashes of the blue sword and as many tentacles severed. Flesh piled between the copies of Bersk. Two whips of the demon struck true, landing squarely on an image, but phased through the bounty hunter—for Bersk was everywhere and nowhere, all at once.

Despite the formidable power of *Mirror Image*, for every tendril cut down, it seemed more sprouted in its place. The swamp became a maelstrom of flesh and steel and blood.

Then the end came. The swamp rumbled, and the brilgura screamed, "*No! Mother! No!*"

The ground around the mutated brilgura split and tore. The ten copies of the bounty hunter fell to their knees. The swamp opened up beneath the demon like quicksand, mud and vines descending into the ground. The brilgura writhed and its tendrils grasped for the ground, desperate to hold on, but its body slipped beneath the surface, and it was gone.

Sudden silence fell over the swamp.

Kevril Bersk's heart was beating in his chest. He breathed deep and let go of the spell. Copies of him disappeared, leaving only the true bounty hunter behind.

~

Bersk willed away *Twitch* and trudged back over to the altar. With the sword gone, his right hand and forearm throbbed steadily beneath his glove.

Idina and Tam met him there. They gathered around Sidac, who was kneeling on the ground, chest heaving. Quiet fear adorned the faces of all three.

The profane altar loomed above them like a great spined tree.

Sidac glanced to the lot of them, his eyes settling on Bersk.

"You did good," the bounty hunter replied with a nod. "Just what you needed to do." Blood dripped down Bersk's right hand and he winced at the stinging pain in his shoulder. His thigh pulsed sharply.

Tam's eyes widened. "Movernus, man! You should've saved some of the beast for the rest of us." The bard waved his hands over the injuries to his shoulders and his leg. "*Sana vulnera suum.*"

Immediately, Bersk felt the skin around the injuries pull taught, as if they were being sutured, and the throbbing pain receded. It wasn't a week's vacation, but he would live.

"Thank you," Bersk mumbled, first to Tam, and then again to Idina.

Idina half-smiled and brushed the frazzled gray hair from her face. "You're on your own next time."

"Now, then," Bersk said, "there's just the matter of the book and the altar—"

The ground quaked beneath them again.

Bersk, Tam and Idina backed away, but as Sidac tried to stand, tendrils reached up from the ground and wrapped around his arms and legs. Sidac screamed. Idina let arrows fly, piercing several arms, but more reached up in their place.

The ground turned to quicksand again as the arms pulled the summoner down into the ground.

"Do something," Idina shouted, but Kevril Bersk just watched.

"The pact demands sacrifice," the bounty hunter replied coldly, "and you did not deliver."

"Please, Bersk!" Sidac shouted, already waist deep in the ground.

Bersk whispered, *"Lectum mortis revelatio,"* and the scene froze. The air grew thick and heavy with magic. The tendrils stopped, though the flesh still pulsed with horrid blood. Tam and Idina stood frozen. An arrow hung in the air—in mid-flight. Bersk's muscles grew tight and burned with exertion though he was standing still—it was next to impossible to move or speak unless you were the caster or the one about to die.

Sidac stared at Bersk. The poor man's eyes glazed over, absent fear, sorrow, or any other emotion.

"Do you regret what you did?"

With eerie calm, Sidac answered, "I regret that I hated the man more than I loved my wife and my son."

He was gone a moment later. Only faint lines and an arrow in the dirt were left to mark Sidac's end. The weight of the spell left the air and again the swamp was quiet.

"By the gods… What was that?" Idina asked, visibly shaken from the spell.

Tam shivered. "A most unpleasant spell. One I'd rather not be near enough to feel again."

Bersk sighed wearily. "It's one of the few spells that can stay a god's hand—for a moment. Doesn't change anything. The poor bastard."

Idina stammered in disbelief. "How could you let him go?" Tam stood beside her, his disbelief turning to disheartenment.

"Sidac's life was forfeit the moment he summoned that demon. Not even my goddess's power is enough to erase a pact. Ariazi owns his soul."

Idina fell to her knees, repeating, "How could you? How could you let him go?"

It took the bounty hunter a few moments longer than he would admit to realize that she was not upset about Sidac's death. The old sellsword had just watched a second life get taken before her eyes, and she was still struggling with the boy's death. For a second time, she had been powerless.

Bersk knelt beside her and put his ungloved hand on her shoulder to comfort her. "Do not think of him as if he was that boy. And do not think of yourself as the *Idina that watched.*" He pointed to the lone arrow that stuck out of the ground. "Your arrows did not stay the demon lord's will, but they are a testament all the same. You are every bit the sellsword of younger days."

Though Idina did not meet his eyes, her breathing slowed, and she nodded reluctantly.

Bersk stood and turned his attention to the altar and the true task, cleansing the damned swamp of Ariazi's influence.

The sellsword knelt in front of the towering, twisting altar and conjured *Twitch.* The discomfort left his hand, and Bersk used the tip of the blade to draw the sigils of order in the dirt, bracing the back of the blade with his left forearm. It took years of practice not just to memorize the design, but to draw the many shapes with steady line and correct intersections. When he finished several minutes later, a dozen interlocking squares and circles adorned the ground, the design every bit as mathematical as it was beautiful.

Then Bersk held Twitch out over the sigil and spoke in the old words.

"By the will of the Gray Queen, I am her hand and her voice.
I stand upon the shoulders of The Dead Prince,
Spurned by the Realm That Has No Name.

We impose the Balance upon this cursed land.”
When he spoke the final line, two other voices overlapped his, and Kevril Bersk knew he was not alone.

Glowing blue dripped from the sword, the same molten consistency that seeped from wounds made by the sword. The blue ether dripped steadily and coalesced into the lines of the sigil. Then the glow retreated from the sword, leaving dull steel in its wake.

And when all the ether had shifted from the sword to the runes, Bersk finished the incantations.

“By the will of the Gray Queen, erase this madness.” the three voices said.

The ground beneath him rumbled as if something were alive and moving beneath the ground. The epicenter shifted from the sigil to the profane altar and the massive structure began to break. Blue oozed from the thorns and then from the cracks that split along its length. Shards and chunks fell, bleeding blue across the ground. Then the tower broke completely, the length of it crumbling and melting into the ground. When it was over, not even blue stain remained.

Bersk held the sword out again over the sigil and the blue ether leapt from its bounds back to the blade, coating and coloring it back to its eerie glow.

“Order come, and Gray Queen’s will be done.”

High in the treetops, Archimedes crowed with satisfaction.

~

Bersk stowed Twitch without ceremony, for he had one thing left to do. He pulled Sidac’s book from the inner pocket of his cloak, careful to touch it with only his left hand, and mused about it. Such an inconspicuous thing, absent markings

and title. The bounty hunter didn't dare read the pages inside—it may have been little more than superstition, but to
gaze upon the words of Ariazi was to invite destruction.

He opened the book *face down* and laid it in the dirt, spoke
the word, "*Inflamma*," and set it ablaze.

"That's it?" Tam asked from behind him. "It's a book for
summoning demons and there's no ceremony?"

Bersk shook his head. "Now, it's just a book, the magic left
with the last of that family." The bounty hunter turned, and
bid Tam and Idina to follow. "Come on, let's give the town the
good news."

He led them out of the swamp. They followed the winding
path of the stones which rose to meet their feet and receded
behind them—all without the magic of Sidac. Bersk doubted
the stones would ever rise again. Tam put on a stoic face in
spite of the horrors they had seen. Idina walked sullenly, still
dwelling on prior loss. Archimedes fluttered through the
branches, never tiring, never growing impatient.

Bersk led them to the first clearing, the one with bones
hanging from the vines. They cut down the bones of the boy
and wrapped his tattered skeleton in a length of cloth from
Tam's pack. Idina insisted on carrying him, and cradled the
lad's remains in her arms.

Kevril Bersk was thankful for that, because touching the
boy's skeleton and feeling the utter emptiness nearly brought
him to tears. Even wearing his glove, there was no hiding the
desolation—no flinching from it. An innocent life given away
in anger and in fear.

~ ~ ~

Chapter 8
Return from Darkness

BY THE TIME they emerged from the swamp, the faintest glimpse of morning sun came over the horizon, bleeding red into the sky. Kevril Bersk had been sore from battle and tired from lack of rest, but it was only when he looked upon the village at the other end of the fields that he felt weary.

Just a bit further, he told himself.

The quiet of the early morning was swept away when they emerged. Shouts rang out from the village, and townsfolk came running. Some bore pitchforks and swords, no doubt ready to seize a demon summoner who was no longer with them.

Halfway across the field, their fervor slowed and most walked in slow march the rest of the way. All but Mrs. Sidac and her son. They ran until they were a few feet away, then Mrs. Sidac fell to her knees. Her son knelt beside her, both sobbing quietly.

Idina walked on, carrying the wrapped bones of the boy and found his mother. Tam stood stoically behind Bersk. Archimedes watched from the treeline.

It wasn't until most of the crowd had gathered that Mrs. Sidac found her voice. "What happened to Sidac, Kevril Bersk? You said you would bring him back to me! You lied to me..."

Hardegen stood behind her, hands clenching softly and unclenching with turmoil and longing on his face. Unable to comfort Mrs. Sidac.

"Your husband died while banishing the brilgura," Bersk said, loud enough for those gathered to hear. "He did what was needed of him. He paid the part of his debt that a man could pay."

Bersk paused, unsure of what to say. Calling Sidac a hero was too much, for no man was a hero that did what was necessary. To overplay his valiance was to downplay his crimes. To say he forgave his wife was a lie. His dying words were a confession of his hate for Hardegen, not his love...

In the end, he fell to the old rule—neither the bounty hunter nor his goddess approved *of ending* on a lie.

Kevril Bersk knelt in front of the orphan son, and bid the widow leave them. Tearfully, she walked to Hardegen and leaned into his arms.

To the boy, Bersk said, "You may be angry, and you have right to be, but do not do as he did. Do not give yourself to evil or to hate, no matter what your intentions. They will consume you.

"At the end... he did not have many words, but his final thoughts were of longing for you and your mother. For all that happened, he loved both of you as if you were his. Remember this, there is no greater love than that which *we choose.*"

The boy nodded slightly and waited, but the bounty hunter had nothing else to say.

The life of Knight, hunter, or sellsword is set upon on all sides by pain and loss and grief, but the truth was that theirs was an easy lot compared to those left in their wake. Bersk would wake tomorrow on the road or in another cursed town. The burden he carried would be miniscule in comparison to those left behind—just as the burden of the dead compared to that of the living that miss them. Mrs. Sidac, the boy, and Hardegen would live here, ever reminded of the tragedy.

Bersk rose and walked past the boy, past the others. He placed a solemn left hand on the shoulder of Idina, who was watching a woman clutching a sack walk alone across the field to the village—the mother of the boy, Sven.

Idina said quietly, "Somebody told me once to take solace in what remains, however little. Even of ourselves. That's precisely why I left that life. If I kept going, eventually there wouldn't be any of me left."

"You did right then. We can't help others if there's nothing left of us."

Idina nodded, taking his meaning. She nodded to the bow on her back and said, "I hope this is the last I know of the old life."

Bersk and Tam walked on through the crowd. The bard was quiet—so much so that Bersk nearly forgot he was there. Tam smiled meekly, his demeanor slowly improving from the swamp. The further they were from the swamp, the better his friend would feel.

They sought Elder Reynolds, who stood meekly in front of Idina, hands clenched together. He said to her, "I'm sorry. Truly, I am. I'm sorry that it took so long, and that I couldn't have done more."

The old hunter clasped Elder Reynold's hands. Idina spoke patiently, in spite of what she'd just been through. "You have every due to be sorry, and I have every right to be angry."

Reynold's face soured. "Please do not punish the town. I will take the blame—"

Idina held up a shaky hand to stay him. "Don't worry, Reynold's. I will continue my vigil to watch over the town, and the people will have my bow. But when I hunt game, I will hunt for myself. I will offer no meat or bounty for a year as recompense."

She walked off solemnly, not waiting to hear Reynold's mumble his thanks. Reynold's sighed and turned to accompany the sellsword and bard back to the village.

Reynolds led them to the ruins of the old noble house—a quiet place amidst the excitement. The old tanner held out a small leather pouch to the sellsword. "It's what we can manage. Silver pieces and some gold."

Bersk took the pouch and slipped it in an inner pocket of his cloak.

"That's it then?" Reynolds asked.

Bersk nodded. "Except I think we promised some of your folk a concert."

Tam met his eyes. Slowly, some of the weariness was leaving the bard. "I'd much prefer some sleep first.

"Thank you. Both of you," Reynold's said, looking both men in the eyes. "You've given us back some peace."

Bersk nodded. "We do what we can."

"It's not much, but this is *our* village." The elder pointed to the outline of the ruins. "When the rest of the continent was burning and Everdeath passed us by, the old noble bastard wasn't content with the normal taxes. He wanted more. More.

Well, we burned his house when Everdeath didn't. Then run him out of town… only gods know where he went.

"I guess my point is that now we can handle ourselves. And if we can't, we know just who to send for."

~

Again, the sellsword and bard found themselves in the stables. Archimedes kept watch from the roof.

Tam was already slumped against a bale of hay. The bard made a show of fluffing up the pile behind his head, then stroked his beard idly, leaving scraps of straw in it. Too tired to mind.

Bersk, on the other hand, had pulled out his lodestone and beckoned for Pater O'Malley, a priest on the other side of the world.

Tam eyed the sellsword. "You don't want to get some shuteye first? Marinade in the straw?"

Bersk shook his head. "By then it will be night on that side of the world."

That was the least of the reasons for speaking with the priest. O'Malley would want to know of the demon and of Ariazi's altar. Whilst, Bersk wanted to know what would become of Santa Anna.

Tam raised his eyebrows, no doubt understanding the sellsword's unspoken meaning.

Bersk added, "I'll be back before you nod off."

The bard chuckled and closed his eyes on the straw. "Doubtful, *Blink*. Doubtful."

The bounty hunter met Tam's tired eyes and smiled. "*Now*, you can call me that."

The lodestone warmed in his hand, signaling that Pater O'Malley accepted his request to meet. Kevril Bersk closed his eyes, thumbed a circle on the face of the lodestone and whispered, *"Ut dominus originis."*

~

The power of the lodestone manifested quickly, silently, without pomp or flair. There wasn't even a sensation of movement or vertigo. Bersk merely opened his eyes and appeared in Pater O'Malley's study—the man who used to be his seigneur.

Santa Anna had once explained to Kev that the lodestones and summoned weapons used similar magic. In short, if swords could feel, Bersk knew what it was like for *Twitch* to appear in his hand.

Kevril Bersk stood in the corner of Pater O'Malley's underground study. The underground portions of the Septriones Church were cut from the ancient stone using old tools instead of magic, resulting in the rooms below ground to look more like caverns. The ceiling was low, scarcely above Bersk's head in certain spots. A single shelf wrapped around the upper wall, holding tomes bound in all colors of leather and script—these were O'Malley's personal collection. Everlit candles floated around the ceiling, light playing off the ripples and ridges like the surface of a darkwater pond. Two bare chairs sat in front of a large ashwood desk in the center of the room; the color gave the illusion that the furniture was merely another part of the cave. O'Malley sat behind it, hunched over *the* holy tome— the Enchiridion.

O'Malley was a wiry, tenacious man, ten years Bersk's senior. Young compared to many priests that lived in the Septriones Church, but already wearing a prominent, graying beard. He wore the black robes of perpetual mourning—customary for all priests and higher ups while they were in *His* abode. The robes were trimmed with gold braids and equally gaudy runes, each with their own tie to chapters of the Enchiridion. The Lord liked his servants to stand out like beacons.

Hanging on the wall behind the priest, was a wide, tattered map of the known world—one passed down from O'Malley's father, and his grandfather. It showed the two sister continents of Eadruin and Ozequn were prominent. To the south, the Frozen Isles spanned the ice-covered sea. Hundreds of pins and tassels adorned the map, each marking the location and date of an altar of Ariazi, the mother of all demons—different color tassels representing different decades.

O'Malley smiled sharply, stood and bowed in custom.

Bersk nodded and sat in one of the slim chairs facing his friend. It was only when he sat that he felt the chill of the underground air—as if it took a moment for his skin to register that he was, in fact, in a different place than moments before.

The priest stowed his fountain pen and pushed the holy tome to the side before giving the hunter his undivided attention.

"So, what news do you bring from the other side of the world, Kevril?"

"I thought you might want to know that the village of Keld wasn't just a brilgura, but also the location of another altar."

O'Malley nodded solemnly, grabbed another pin from an ornate box on his desk. Then he rose and placed a marker on the other side of the world.

"Forgive me for prying," Bersk said, "But they look more numerous as of late."

O'Malley sat and leaned on the arm of the chair. "You would be right. The bishops like to think that it means that we're putting out more fires—that things are getting better. Anyone worldly knows that's not the case. In other words, we're in need of hunters."

"No, thanks. Enough people still think I work for you."

The priest jested. "Are they wrong?"

Bersk smirked and shook his head. "No."

The bounty hunter wanted to say, *and that's the problem*. He had quit, but still owed so many favors that he still had one foot in the door. He let it go.

It was *the people* he liked at the Church, the people that he still helped out. The people that he still cared about. He didn't work for the Church of First Light, or believe in their mission, or much *like it* anymore.

Which led to the question he really wanted to ask: "Has anyone talked to her yet?"

O'Malley's face soured. "They can't find her. I don't need to tell you how that looks."

"Can you blame her?"

"Yes. Yes, I can." O'Malley replied. "She's a *bishop*. All she needs to do is put the rumors to rest. Her record is impeccable, but she's a fool if she thinks she can merely hide behind her title."

Bersk's mind reeled with possibilities, and he rapped gloved fingers hard on the chair to silence his thoughts.

"Whatever you're thinking, *don't*," the priest said.

The bounty hunter shrugged. "I wasn't."

O'Malley glared at him.

Bersk pointed a gloved finger at him. "Whatever it is, whatever part they *think* she's playing, she's innocent. She's not a part of this conspiracy. Just because some fat tailor throws out a name—"

"And if she's not part of the conspiracy, then she'll have nothing to worry about. It's that simple."

Bersk shook his head. "That's where we disagree. However this started, it's turned into a witch-hunt. Unfounded accusations are the death of people, O'Malley."

"Maybe it's better you aren't here for this," the priest muttered, rubbing his temple.

"I tried to leave."

"Yes. Yes. I remember."

Kevril Bersk sighed. It always inevitably came up—his leaving the Church. O'Malley felt he'd lost a friend. Bersk felt as if he'd lost several. The Church felt as if they'd lost a weapon. Either way, Bersk was still doing what he did best: Hunting.

Silence fell between the two men—uncomfortable silence, as of late.

Bersk said quietly, "Keld was a little town that Sircius Everdeath forgot. It was untouched—*untouched*, I tell you. Come to find out, it was only because one of the villagers called on Ariazi to protect them. Then there's the conspiracy inside the Church...

"Some days I can keep going without problem," Bersk continued. "Some days it's a sense of duty or righteousness. Other days I don't know how to keep going, but I can't bring myself to stop. I wish I didn't care, but there's good people that get ground up out there. Good people that get ground up in here, too. Pulverized by gods and demons, kingdoms and the Church—by forces beyond ourselves. How do you reconcile that, Pater? How do *you* reconcile that?"

O'Malley replied, "We do what we must, priest and hunter, alike. But a man can only do so much on his own. We are all bound by powers and wills greater than our own. I know you're worried about Santa Anna, but you must keep the faith."

The priest pulled out a small ornate bottle of salve and set it on the desk.

Bersk chuckled. "Kicking me out so soon?"

O'Malley shook his head and tried to keep the melancholy off his face. "Doesn't do you good to stay here too long. Besides, this is really why you're here, right?"

The bounty hunter shifted uneasily in his seat, gloved hand itching with discomfort. "If there was some other place I could go for relief… I would still visit." He knelt in front of the desk, removed his glove, and placed his right arm down before the priest.

O'Malley put on his own thin gloves and muttered words of healing over the bottle. "*Let go the tired maladies of skin. Let this tonic reduce the chaotic mix of man and blade, until this hand hath no difference from the other, and his fortitude returned therein.*"

O'Malley spoke the old words and poured the salve over Bersk's gnarled forearm and worked it into his skin, starting from the elbow and moving downward. It was a tedious process, punctuated by occasional mutterings by the priest.

Over the years, Kevril Bersk had gone to healers, mages, and holy men, but nothing short of the Church's particular salve helped. It deadened the pain and the sensitivity. And that was all it did. There was no cure, save giving up the sword, and to Bersk that was not an option.

Sometimes he could go two missions between applications.

Neither spoke until O'Malley worked his way down to Kevril's fingers.

"It looks worse and worse each time you come here," the priest said.

"I'll live the natural lifespan of a sellsword then."

"That sword is going to be the death of you."

"Just work your magic," Bersk replied flatly.

Twitch was going to be the death of him—whether by withering or by trade. But one did not give up a gift like that until it was necessary.

Kevril Bersk, caught between a goddess he cannot deny and the Church he cannot leave. Because of this, his sword hand was marred and painful—to remind him that in a world where men were bound to powers beyond them, it was not comfortable to serve more than one.

Bersk was only sad that people like Tam, Santa Anna, and O'Malley had to watch him suffer.

When the last of the salve was gone, Bersk donned the glove again. Both men stood and regarded each other.

There were a dozen things that could've passed between them—perhaps more that *should* have passed between them. But men have an even harder time with depth and sincerity of emotions than sellswords.

Perhaps that was why Bersk preferred the company of the bard to the priest as of late. Tam could put to song and story all the things that neither of them could say in humble conversation.

Besides, this was not the last time that Kevril Bersk would see Pater O'Malley, and so he was not bound by the Gray Queen's tenet of ending with honesty.

Bersk merely nodded to his friend. "Until next time, Pater."

O'Malley half-smiled. "Until next time."

Kevril Bersk thumbed a circle on the face of the lodestone. "*Ad locum meum.*"

~

Bersk returned to the stables in Keld, on Ozequn, in the same silent manner with which he left. He laid down in the straw, and thought of walking in the church courtyard beside Santa Anna before drifting off. He slept until midday, when both he and Tam were awoken by the sound of a flute or a recorder.

Both the sellsword and bard woke groggily, propped themselves up and listened to the young woman's playing. Through the raven's eyes on the roof, Bersk could see a small crowd gathered again. Today she played a slow waltz and Tam's head swayed to the melody.

"We should probably be going soon, shouldn't we?" the bard asked.

Bersk nodded. "After your encore and after we get some food in us, yes."

They rose and walked the village street. Though the bounty hunter's stomach growled, he couldn't deny the bard or the young freckled woman their last duet. Both she and the small group around her positively beamed as Tam approached. So, brunch waited while art was satisfied.

Tam swung the lute from his back, leaned beside her on the side of the hut and followed her lead through the slow waltz. One would think that both her and Tam had played together many times before for how well they played together.

Bersk stayed in the back of the small crowd, attempting to keep a stoic demeanor. He thought again of the skill it took to accompany another musician as Tamren Jorbough did, and the comparison to counterspelling. Kevril Bersk may have had a heavier hand in banishing the brilgura and Ariazi's altar, but that was akin to counterspelling too—he had taken away the demon, the altar, a woman's husband and a boy's father. Bersk could not assuage their family, nor the mother of the boy taken by the brilgura.

Tamren Jorbough was leaving magic in his wake. The young woman would be all the better for it. The town would be better for it.

Such was the nature of the world. Destruction was easier than rebuilding, harmful magic easier to learn than healing magic—why rebuilding took longer and healing mages were so few.

And while his friend Tam walked beside him, Kevril Bersk could pretend that he was just as much a part of that magic.

END

NEXT TIME ON
The Sword of the Gray Queen
Book 2:

Hive of the Formicae
Available October 2022

Spoiler–Free excerpt from
Hive of the Formicae

Archimedes perched in one of the trees at the edge of the forest, just above the wandering patrol. Bersk and Tam met them at the edge.

Both of the patrol were young men, wearing the standard brown uniform with orange trim, stained with flecks of mud or possibly blood.

"Who goes there?" one of them shouted.

Tam and Bersk stepped out from the brush with hands raised and absent weapons so as not to alarm them.

All the better, because both patrolmen were young and looked shaken. Both kept hands on the pommels of their swords.

"Sorry to alarm you, lads. It is I, Tamren Jorbough the poet, returned to speak with your Captain Henring. I've brought the monster hunter I spoke of."

The stouter young man with a bit of fuzz for a mustache nodded to his companion and both relaxed. "We didn't expect you for another two days." He sighed heavily. "It doesn't matter. Captain Henring and the others will be pleased."

He looked Kevril Bersk up and down and nodded again. "I don't know much about monsters, but you look the part of a hunter, sir."

"Why lad, this here is Kevril Bersk, former Knight of the Order—"

"Bersk is fine," the hunter said narrowing his eyes. "No need for formalities."

"All the same, sir—eh, Bersk," the soldier said. "We'll show you the way."

Bersk and Tam followed the soldiers, while Archimedes flew ahead to the camp.

To be continued October 2022

Thank you for Reading

I hope you enjoyed reading this story as much as I enjoyed writing it.

If you did, I would massively appreciate a short review on Amazon or your favorite book website. Reviews are crucial for any author, and a starred review or even just a line or two can make a huge difference.

It's especially true for the start of a series. Thanks and I hope you enjoy the next one!

Looking for more dark fantasy stories in this universe?

The Sword of the Gray Queen is one series in a dark fantasy universe, *Eluthiya*.

Tales from Another World is an ongoing short story series containing stories about sorcerers, druids, mortals, gods, thieves, and all other manner of Terrans from all over the twin continents.

Among other stories, will be snippets of Sircius Everdeath's crusade that nearly destroyed the world! So, if you're interested, be sure to check out the ongoing series.

And if you liked the action and adventure in this story, be sure to check out the ongoing monthly serial **A Battleaxe and a Metal Arm.** It's the adventure of a lifetime… or several!

About the Sword of the Gray Queen

It's hard to point to the exact moment of genesis for an idea. Most of the time, we writers might only have the vaguest notion of where an idea came from—if we have any idea at all!

The Secret of Milton Boska came from a random winter's day. *D3H Repurposed* from a thought experiment about holding onto memories. *Amber in the Real World* was a slow-burn version of The Matrix. *A Battleaxe and a Metal Arm* was originally an idea for a D&D campaign. *Tales from Another World* and *Eluthiya* was my first attempt to make a universe that made sense.

The Sword of the Gray Queen came from fan fiction.

Originally, *TWOFGQ* was going to be The Witcher Kills Cereal Box Mascots.

Count Chocula would've been a lich or a vampire. The Rice Krispie Elves were going to be a trio of hags. Tony the Tiger, obviously a weretiger. Sonny the Cuckoo would've been something like a dinosaur/terror bird. The Trix Rabbit—the murderous rabbit from Monty Python and the Holy Grail. Lucky the Leprechaun—murderous leprechaun/gnome. Captain Crunch, obviously a murderous pirate… You get the idea.

Before you ask, I never actually wrote anything out—I never even got past the brainstorming part. I just liked the idea of a completely serious Geralt of Rivia hunting down these ridiculous monsters. I didn't even figure out whether I wanted to make it a comedy where the mascots were animated and just trying to survive, or whether the mascots would be monster-ized versions of themselves and the idea would be played straight.

I was playing around with the latter idea when it occurred to me that I really enjoyed the idea of a Sword & Sorcery style romp about monster hunting. Don't get me wrong, I like Epic Fantasy, but I felt like a small POV/cast was perfect for this type of story.

Anyway, that's the genesis *of The Sword of the Gray Queen*. If any of you out there write fan fiction and actually take the time to write out a version of The Witcher Kills Cereal Box Mascots, send the link to me. I want to read it.

And in case you were wondering, yes, the Honey Smacks Dig 'Em Frog is the Brilgura.

Connect with the Author

If you want to stay up to date on the latest about Samuel's publishing news and blog, check out his website and consider signing up for his monthly newsletter.

www.SamuelFlemingBooks.com

Samuel can also be found on Reddit, Tiktok, and Facebook.

Samuel Fleming is a Science Fiction and Fantasy author.

He grew up in Maryland, spending most of his time swimming and writing. Swimming gave him a lot of time to daydream, so the two hobbies complemented each other well. Idle day dreams turned into stories, some of which stuck with him for years. These days he swims a little less and writes a lot more.

He loves a good story no matter the medium: Books, TV, video games, comics, tabletop RPG's, or podcasts—most of which he attempts to share with his wife and three kids, and occasionally on his blog.